Chronicles of the Forgotten One

MERLIN LYNAA

2022

Novel published under pen name: Merlin Lynaa
Editing address: Merlin Gray, Balleroy sur Drôme, France
Editing name : Foxdown Editing
ISBN : 9791097524203

For reproduction, adaptation or translation rights, please contact Merlin through merlingideon.com

My thanks go to those of you who believed in my work and supported it through its crowd funding on Ulule.com.

Thank you to my amazing fiancée Ye-Ul

Thank you to my dear friend and colleague Judy

Thank you to my brother from another mother Khaled

Thank you to my friend and colleague Abigail

Thank you to my writing buddy Nell

Thank you to Zalphos for your amazing support

Thank you to Elann for your kindness

Thank you to Eponyme for supporting my work

Thank you to Silane for your kind support

Thank you to my friends and students Navy and Line for your support too!!

Without all of you, this project would have been a lot more complicated to keep alive and even more difficult to bring to its conclusion.

Cross-Gen

A strange ad. in a strange place

Dear reader, my name is Haiylen, this is the beginning of my story and hey, I've got no idea why I'm writing it other than pure boredom. I suppose I should tell you more about the protagonist you're going to be following for the duration of this story: me. I'm currently 15 years old, graduated from high school but too young to go to university – I've got to be 16 for that – and I'm what is known as a 'pupil of the nation'. In simpler words, I'm an orphan living in a French orphanage in Southern France not too far out from the port city of Toulon.

I was found at the age of 8, on a wooden chest filled with clothing and useful stuff for me to live, a letter to the person who would find me saying my name was Haiylen, and enough cash to last a while. You might wonder why there was a letter telling whoever what my name was, well that's because I could not even remember that when they found me.

Strangely, I could speak but it was the wrong language, I only spoke English.

After I was found, I was immediately reported to the police and was then questioned, examined by a doctor and finally taken to a shelter. It was located on the way out of the city and, within minutes of arriving there, someone came to pick me up. Speaking English to me in a kind voice, they took care of me, and then I was taken to the orphanage in a nearby town called Cuers. The drive was not long, strangely I remember that really well and especially the next part. When I arrived at the orphanage, my life basically became hell. For every word of English I spoke, the French translation was screamed back at me; I was not to speak my language here. The matron of the place took the letter, read it, and burnt it. She also took all my stuff, threw it on a table in the commons and told the other tenants to take all they wanted but to leave my, and I quote, 'disgusting male underwear'. Only then did I realise that there were only 3 boys for 23 girls in residence. Obviously, the bank notes that came with the letter disappeared never to be seen again.

I was first put in the attic, on my own, on a decrepit quilt on the ground. However, the next day the social services came to register me and I could thus not be shunned away. I obviously told them that the money had been taken but was not believed; I was too young and did not even know where I was born. They created my identity from pictures and scraps of information I randomly made up. Thus, to the officials, I was 8 when they found me, I guessed this based on the clothing sizes all saying 8Y, my name was as above and I was born in England. No town or anything was given and they told me they were trying to find my parents and had put out a request to Interpol to look into my name.

That evening was the first time I got hit, it was so blindingly painful that I very nearly lost consciousness on the spot. The matron, of whom we simply knew the name Madlain, or Mad as the other residents called her, had struck me across the back with a wet mop. It was winter. You can surely imagine how cold that was.

Following that day, I found out that corporal punishment was a norm in this place and that nigh on anything deserved the matron's wrath. I was to remain up in the attic area with my roommates, Jenny, Laura, and Luis. The first night I was in a different part, a storage room. My roommates are all around my age, Jenny was found in a car boot on a motorway shoulder, the car had been abandoned with her. Laura was left out in a forest to die, at the age of 3. As for Luis, he was simply dropped off here as a 7-month-old infant. Of all of us, I had the strangest name, past or lack thereof, and was also immediately the most hated by Mad.

After my first month in the place, I found out that we are supposed to homeschool ourselves and that was when I started really learning French as well as a lot of other things. As all the textbooks we had were for 12-year-olds and older, that's where we all started and the older kids tried to help us figure things out. It was nearly 2 years later that I realised how fast I was learning things, I should have still been struggling with the 12- or 13-year-old stuff but was already in the 16-year-old stuff. This, for some reason, was only met by more wrath from the matron until exam time came. She refused that I go to pass the exam I clearly had the knowledge for so I sneaked out and followed the others into town. Sadly, without the correct paperwork, I could not do the tests and that evening I fell unconscious under Mad's blows.

When I woke up sometime in the evening, back in the loft, I found myself tucked into bed, with all wounds freshly bandaged. Jenny, Laura and Luis had made us a bed on the ground and were sleeping against me. It took another two years to convince Mad to let me take exams, by which time I had worked through all the available textbooks and needed to do the high school graduation exam. As I had not done the other prerequisite exam, I had to first pass it and thus waste a full year. My results were almost all perfect in all subjects, much to Mad's horror, as her punch told my back. We had a silent celebration in the loft that evening and I was kissed for the first time, by both Laura and Jenny. It was just a peck but it was also the only congratulations gift they had for me. That night, we fell asleep in a heap on the ground, all four of us hugging each other.

I finally did the graduation exams a year later. I was the youngest pupil in the room at 14. This time, I registered for as many tests as I could regardless of possible results. I failed all the ancient languages and history but got perfect scores on all the sciences and languages. The evening I received my results was the second time I fell unconscious under the matron's fist. You would think that a boy of 14 would be stronger than that, well she is huge. And if ever she reads this, I'll be dead meat. I forgot to mention, Jenny had also got her results but she was congratulated, perks of being a girl. Laura was being adopted three days later so she had been moved out of the loft to a vacant room on the first floor. Luis was nowhere to be seen that night.

The sad story goes on: Luis, after being repeatedly maltreated by Mad had head trauma. She only told us three weeks after his sudden absence that he had died. This led to an investigation of the orphanage but Mad prepared for that, she threatened to kill anyone who would say anything against her methods and she even paid off two of the officers to make it sound like Luis had been pushed in the stairs. That dear reader, was when we figured out just how urgently we needed to find a way out of here. None of the older kids ever came back and the adoptees did not even write to their old roommates.

A few days before my made up birthday, when I was to turn 15, the local mayor came around to give us all unlimited access to the town library. He also made it clear that it was a mandatory thing to go once a week for various reasons. Mad hated this but he seemed to have his eye on her, so she just told us all that not a word was to be said to strangers. The day of my birthday was my day to go to the library, the best present ever. I walked there with Jenny and we were planning on getting books to study until we were of age for university. That was the plan until we found out about the computers. In 2013, what makes a computer special? Well, everything, if you've never seen one before. That was when I found one of my biggest interests to date, technology. I borrowed four books on computers and programming which Jenny supplemented with her book loan authorisation and added for four others. Between the two of us, we had a lot of heavy reading until next week.

Why am I telling you all this, mainly to explain how two 15-year-old kids got onto the dark web in a small-town library one winter evening? It was just before they were going to close, between the two of us, we had managed to do all the steps and were on the dark web. The first search I typed in was 'how to run away from home' very stupid but it had loads of results. The best one to me was 'burn the place down' followed by a recipe for a Molotov cocktail… Needless to say, I did not click on that. We kept all our steps ready and left lots of them still running when we went back to the orphanage that night. The week of waiting to go back and explore more was horrible. It was snowing but we were forbidden to play, three more kids were dropped off, all girls. We are currently 25 girls and me, one guy. Well, I mean, I guess I'm a guy even if I often wear girl clothes as there are not really boy ones that fit me. To be blunt, I've never really felt much like a guy either and Mad has all the girls, and me, taking the pill. Yeah, she knows it's bad for me but doesn't care. Because of that, I've never really developed much maleness per se. When we went back to the library the next week, it only took a few minutes to have the two computers we were on connected to the dark web. As I was searching for anything about the place we were all living in, to see if there was a way of attracting attention to it, I found the ad. One cold and wet winter day, with my one and only friend, in a horrible yellow chair at the town library, I found the ad. for Cross-Gen. Or more specifically, the Cross-Gen program.

It reads like as follows, and yes, I memorised it because that was yesterday and I copied it all down. Jenny thinks it's a hoax but I'm really not so sure.

'Do you want to become more? More than you ever were and surely more than any can imagine you would become? Well, we can help you achieve that. If you are between 14 and 17 then our program is for you. Make your way to 23 rue Neuve, 13,000 Marseille on any Tuesday morning at 10 p.m. for the bus to our facilities. No parents are allowed. If you can't go there, call +9871 231 452 1290, and we will pick you up at a place of our convenience near your location.' What a strange number, I found out that was a satellite phone and was registered to no one. Obviously, I wanted to go, it was a way out, a sigh of freedom. I convinced Jenny to join me and soon we started packing bare essentials and got ready to go, all behind the matron's back. We have to sneak into the office to call Cross-Gen and, when we will, things are either going to be horribly difficult, impossible, or maybe it is all a hoax.

Well, mission accomplished. I don't know if I'll be able to relate this properly but basically Mad snores a lot so it's easy to know when it's safe to move around. We managed to get into the office, call the number and it was not even a fake, they are coming to get us in 3 days, Tuesday, on their way back from Marseille. Jenny is very worried about all of this but I think it's our only safe bet. We can't run away; the officials will just bring us back because we are underage. There is no way we can wait any longer with the way Mad treats us. So, when we told the Cross-Gen people we are orphans, the person on the other side simply said 'perfect'.

Making our way out of the orphanage was not easy. Although Mad was asleep, she had locked the place up just as much as she usually does, in other words, a lot. We ended up going through a window and running from there to the outskirts of town. The bus is to get us in about 20 minutes so, for now, we are huddled together with our hopes up.

A Bus and the Loss of a Name

The bus just got here, a few minutes late. We were ushered inside and found a few other kids looking at us. The driver told us we had one more stop and then it was a straight line to Cross-Gen France. As soon as the bus started up again so did the chatting but that was short-lived as we were told to be quiet. 'You are all currently without any paperwork, invisible to the outside world and will be deleted from any record as soon as we arrive. You will not use your names but be given a code and that will be your only identity until you leave the facility for good.' Said the one supervisor dude. Jenny huddled closer to me, and no dear reader we are not together just close friends who have shared a room for ages. She softly spoke into my ear: 'I know this was a way out, but do you really think it's a good idea? I feel like it's more of a prison.' I simply nod, I have no idea but we needed to get out of the orphanage, Mad was trying everything to clip our wings and make us want to die.

I must have fallen asleep because it's now starting to light up outside and we are in the middle of forest land. I think we are nearly at our destination. Jenny is asleep, her head on my lap. She is small, 1m55 and only about 44 kg. Her shoulder length straight black hair is covering her slightly angular face. I brush her hair back with my hand and then lightly shake her to wake her up. Just in time as the bus comes to a halt.

'Kids, we are here. Leave your stuff behind, walk out of the bus single file and straight into the building. You will be delt with there. And no talking!' That last part was yelled rather than spoken and that seems to be the norm around here. It's not as bad as Mad but it feels like people really just love shouting.

We did as we were told and were walked into the building, through a triple door gateway that was clearly designed to keep people in or out. They lined us up against the wall and took pictures of us, then blood (3 vials each) and then we were ordered to strip. Yes, you read that right, no fancy welcome just a 'Remove any clothing and accessories here and now.' After that, we had to walk single file into a scanner thing and, on the other side, we were handed a pair of track pants and a tee-shirt, no underwear. As you can imagine, there was some complaining at the strip order, especially considering the lack of respect towards the various genders; well, it was met with a slap or a punch in the stomach depending on how long the complaining lasted. On our tee-shirts, they walked up with a marker and wrote a code number, mine is YC503 and Jenny who is right in front of me is XC502.

Things were pretty intense after that; we were taken to three rows of tables with people in lab coats on the other side of them and then asked a load of questions. Things such as 'What is your favourite colour?' or 'What animal do you want to be?' and other even more obscure things like 'how do you prefer to have sex, violent or soft?' and it got worse to the point where they asked me, 'would you kill or rape your best friend for personal satisfaction?' I mean what the hell was that question there for in the first place. I obviously said no and told them that it was a horrible thing to ask to which I was told: '503, shut up unless you are told to speak'. The questions went on for some time until we were all done and then moved into another room, a dorm.

I can't really explain the size of it other than by saying that it's comparable to an A380 aeroplane hangar. It is currently half full of bunk beds and along the wall are open showers and other sanitary things for one part. The other half of the room has desks and chairs as well as a lot of equipment but looking at it a little closer, there is a fence between this side and that one. Our beds are bunks and again they are not gender specific, just numbered which thankfully means I'm near Jenny. The ceiling is almost only huge panels of either glass or plastic but we can see day rising. I guess we won't have any free time to sleep considering the other residents are waking up. I'm still slightly shocked at the treatment and, I must admit, I wish I had not dragged my only friend into this mess with me. No one is moving from the area around their beds towards the showers or anything else and none of them is talking either. In that respect, my group sticks out like a sore thumb, they are all talking. Only Jenny, myself and another girl are actually quiet. The girl is looking around, she seems frightened and, while looking at her, I'm actually wondering: how many of us chose to come here and how many were forced. Only a few minutes later, a loud bell rings before a voice speaks nearly as loud. 'A new group of 17 has joined the facility today. Do not welcome them or try to be friends, that's not why you're here. Number 498 through 515, head over to the shower area, do not wear any clothes or you will be striped and not given others until next week. Others, head over to the medical zone.'

Those numbers are my group and the orders clearly state we are supposed to undress. As we only have two pieces of clothing, it does not take long. The girl I mentioned earlier silently joins Jenny and myself, she is 501 so just before us. She looks at me and half blushes, I try to smile but don't want her to be shy, it's not fun to be nude in front of strangers. We walk over to the open shower area and as we do water comes on. It's too hot but we are told to get clean or they will use a high-pressure hose. Two of the girls from the group walk towards the showers in the garments we are given. As they get here, a guard, not sure if male or female considering the build, walks up behind them with a knife and cuts the cloths right off the one while ripping them off the other. 'You'll be naked until next week now, well done!' She says; for yes, it is a woman.

Under boiling water we clean, then stand under a dryer and then we are told to go back, to get dressed and go to a door on the far left of the room.

Far Too Many Needles

Now, that's a cool chapter title, isn't it? If only it were not so accurate. We were finally back to being dressed, other than the two girls who had defied the order to go to the showers naked, they were huddling under blankets from their beds. They then shepherded us all into a small room off the side of the dorm area where we got seated at a row of tables and waited. A guy walked in and the guards looked down, I guess he's the boss around here. 'Welcome to Cross-Gen. My name Martin Heryoung but that is of no importance to you lot. I'm the head researcher in this facility and also the CEO of the company. You'll see me only on days of choosing such as today or, in rare cases, if I feel like personally inspecting your progress. So, as you saw when you found the ad. to come here, our promise is to make you more than you are and even more than you can imagine. Obviously, that was click bait and you all fell for it.' That explains a lot and raises a few noises of discontent. Those immediately get answered by a slap on the back from the guards. 'As I was saying, click bait. You're all smart or stupid enough to have found that ad. but you still went and followed it. In other words, you're all desperate for something and I believe we have just that or at least we will when we find the key.' What the fuck is this guy on about now? That's basically all that goes through my mind and I think everyone else's too. 'The key is a reference to unlocking Pandora's box and, in our case, it is about unlocking the human DNA. As the name of the company says, we are doing cross-species genetics and you lot are the test subjects.' This time only silence and a few unhappy gulps. I mean damned... That's not what I had bet on but I guess it will be an interesting death. 'Today you will be quizzed and then we will inject you with an amount of animal DNA. It will then be catalysed onto yours in three weeks' time. I'm not going to get technical here but know that it's carried by a virus of our design but is not contagious.' Great, so he wants to make chimaeras out of a bunch of lost kids, what a strange occupation. 'You will then be observed for 6 months until your next choosing day. If you don't want to proceed with the program, well too bad. Oh, and before I leave, young ladies.' He looks at the two who are under their blanket. 'Make sure to follow every order you hear and even the ones you don't, my people are authorised to damage you in basically any way they see fit so long as it doesn't interfere with the experiment.' He says no more and leaves the room.

A bunch of white-garbed people walk in a sit in front of each of us. We are then asked loads of questions, many straight to the point such as 'What animal do you want to be.' I answer that I want a combination between an arctic fox and a wolf with some lizard for the healing abilities and maybe a little other stuff too. The doc looks at me surprised and then asks if it really does not bother me to be a lab rat. To that I reply: 'I'll rather be a lab rat than a dead rat.' The questions go on for quite some time until their little file is full and they walk out. The guards stare us down as if daring us to make a move. It's so silent you'd think we are holding our breaths. What seems like an eternity and a half later, probably only a few minutes, the lab people walk back in with briefcases and come and sit in front of us again. We are then ordered to remove our top garments and lay on our stomachs across the table. The next thing I feel is a horrible stabbing pain on my spine. The reflex to jerk seems to be predictable as the doc has her hand on my neck and pushes my face into the table. 'You're not to move 503!' She says. The same stabbing pain comes, again and again, seventeen times, down my spine and over my shoulder blades. When she stops that part, I'm told to sit up and give my writing arm. I put forth my left arm and next thing I know the doc has a tattoo needle above my arm. I finally see the syringes, all 17 of them, perfectly aligned in the case with long thin needles. Just as I look at them, I feel the pain flair up in my arm and see the doc tattoo me. 'YC503-FWTL-D,' it says. We are literally rats to them; they even tattoo us to make sure we know that. When that bit is done, with our arms nice and red, we are told to get dressed and leave, no cream on the fresh tattoo or anything like that.

When you think your day can't get any worse, just remember, everything and anything can happen. We get back to our bunks and are told to make our beds and head to the eating area. That gives me just enough time to ask Jenny what her tattoo says. 'XC502-PFTC-D.' I suppose the four letters are the animals they injected us with. 'Are you okay?' I ask her. She nods and looks at my arm. 'How many injections did they give you? I got 19.' To which I reply that I had two less. Our conversation stops there as we are ordered to the eating area a second time. Now, what can possibly be worse than up to 20 needles in your spine and a tattoo?

Well, have you ever heard of the word 'splooch?' That's what the older residents call the food here, it's based on the noise it makes when hitting the tray. As it's our first meal, they actually bothered to tell us what it is. You know that strange stuff they feed babies that looks like it's predigested and spat out, well this is worse than that. They designed this splooch to look like puke, smell like synthetic fruit and taste like over-boiled egg. The explanation plaque reads as follows:

'The high nutrient base food is designed for the sole purpose of giving your body all that it needs. It contains high amounts of protein, sugars, vitamins and minerals to make sure you will need only one meal per day. You will have 25 minutes to eat and if you refuse to, we will employ any force necessary to make you eat.'

Basically, we don't have a choice to eat and if you're wondering like I did what force means, let me explain what I just saw. One of the residents at another table was not eating and their table's time ran up, the other left with their bowls empty. Two of the guards or supervisors or whatever they are walked up to him and told him he had a minute. Just as he said no, a funnel was produced, stuffed unto his throat and the splooch poured down it. As much as he gagged, it still stayed down. They then lifted him, kicked him behind the knees and told him to get back to his bunk. That was all the insight we needed to finish our disgusting stuff without further ado. It slips down your throat and feels as horrible as a runny nose but with synthetic egg taste.

From there on, our day becomes a bit of a blur of action. We have 6 hours of monitored physical activities to which no one is really fully adapted, not even the older residents. I'm actually quite surprised to see that the guards leave us to help each other out during this part. I thus overheard the fact that there had been five failed attempts to leave the place and three had resulted in a general message to announce their deaths. I also found out that although quite rare, some do die here. Oh, and one last interesting thing that I actually see as good news, once we are no longer the new group, we are allowed to spend time with the other rats. Yep, rats, that's what the older residents call each other. I overheard something else but I'm not sure if I heard right. It seems that no one remains in this hanger building for more than one year, right after the second catalysis they get moved elsewhere. It would seem that some leave at that time too because the bus is often heard on such days.

From the hours of sport, we are told to strip and go to the showers. Any of the rats that have been here for more than my group just get naked and go. That's the first time I realise that none of them has any body hair, head hair is left alone or trimmed but bodies are close shaven or something similar. Girls and boys are all together and march off to the showers so we quickly join them, leaving our clothes, just as they did, in bins by the sports area. I'm really not used to seeing so many naked bodies but that does not seem to faze anyone in the older groups, only us newbs. I'm even surprised to see the solidarity between them, passing soap and washing backs. We are later told that not cleaning properly is punishable. I mean they could have just summed it up and said that if we don't do any of the things they tell us to, they will force us.

Our day ended with a fresh set of clothes, other than for the two girls who are still not allowed to wear any for 6 days, and then we were given one hour of in-group social time before lights out.

During the social time, I met Amber, Hollie and Saphyr, three of the girls I had been intrigued by. Amber and Hollie are the two who are cloths forbidden and Saphyr is the discrete one I saw on the first day.

Sleep comes easily that night as I lie in bed, my arm over the edge of the bunk, stroking Jenny's hair as she sleeps. And no dear reader, there is still nothing happening and I doubt there will ever be.

You thought that was bad?

Yep, here goes another chapter of your favourite main character, YC503, complaining about his life.

It took only three days for me to find out what the last letter on my tattoo means. D, for December, the month when I get my next choice of DNAs to be injected with. Though before that happens, I need to get the previous ones catalysed, FIVE TIMES. They actually explained catalysis to us before just doing it as they want us to self-observe any changes that could happen. Apparently, each group gets different amounts of catalysis processes but all only stay here for a year at most.

In the Cross-Gen definition, catalysis represents the medical act of removing all the unused DNA we have and forcing the animal DNA to bond in their place. Currently, they've successfully done this to all of us a number of times but no changes have happened in our minds or bodies. The process of catalysis is a damned painful one, though. As they need the catalysing agent to reach each of our cells, we are injected on each leg, arm, down our spine and into the back of our skulls with more than 50 needles. Sorry, I can't be precise on that but I fell unconscious after the first twenty or so; some of them are huge. As soon as that's done, we had to go into a special room where they boosted the oxygen levels and air pressure to more than triple the normal values. Sixty-five percent pure 0_2 and a pressure of 3.2 bars. I only know this because for some strange reason they actually tell us what they are doing.

I'll have to admit, I was out of it for a while in there the first time, the second time and now even the fifth time, but I might be able to tell you what it feels like this time. There must be something injected into the air because we all end up kind of hyperactive and crazy in there. I mean two of the girls randomly started hugging everyone while laughing, one guy tried to kiss me and then went on to hug me anyway. I've no idea what their reason for submitting us to this is but I managed to figure out that it lasts about a full day. We leave after food, get injected, go into the room and get back in time for wake-up and food again.

It may seem strange to you that they tell us so much about what is happening inside the room, what they are doing to us and so on but they have a logical reason for that too, it's to ascertain any changes. They are so worried something might actually happen to us and that they will miss it that they tell us what sort of signs to look out for in our thoughts, bodies and so on. I mean what do they expect? That someone is going to grow a tail and it won't be visible for all of us to see? We are walking around naked nearly half of the day so I'm pretty sure they would spot a change if there were one.

If you remember what I told you last time about our bodies and how they treat us, well, let me give you some more juicy details on that matter. So, we do six hours of sport every day, weights, running around the room, stretching, cardio and even a little combat sort of sport. Anyone who does not complete all the given exercises is forced to do push-ups; not so bad you might think, well let's just say that it's all we end up doing in the last hour as no one can complete the jumps and other things they set for us. Sport aside, we are given trimmers once a month and told to cut each other's hair. Of course, some do this better than others but the guards don't really care what we do other than for a few details. We are not allowed to have hair covering our ears or to have any on the back of our necks, it must be cut off. Thus, we all kind of look like Vikings with hair on the top of our head shaven on the sides and tied above our necks. Yes, I have long hair now, I asked Amber not to cut it short other than where we are obliged to. I thus found out that I have curly hair which I had never known as Mad buzz cut my hair each time it grew even a bit.

As for our body hair, pubic and everywhere else, there is a hair removing agent in the body soap we are given and it makes all hair come off. It doesn't work so well on newcomers so the first week they actually gave us razors and told us to shave everything off in the shower area after which they hosed us down. Yep, lovely, right? And high pressure at that on nice raw skin.

Since we got here, three more groups arrived on our side of the hangar and two groups left out the other. The ones who left all seemed to be happy to cross the boundary in which they have been confined for a full year.

For my group, known currently as the 'December group', we still have nearly six months left in this place. That is if we are actually freed after the first year or if it's a general execution of the useless rats. And yes, as you can imagine, it is currently December and thus our day of choice is tomorrow. This time they went a little more high-tech, they made us line up by a set of tablets upon which we had scroll down lists and a 3D render of what each choice will give. By typing in our ID code, it put in all the things that we already had and gave a render of what we should currently look like. In my case, well here goes a little description:

Green eyes with slit irises elongated eyelids and slightly slanted. Pointy ears on the top of my head with long hair between them. Angular facial bones, pointy even I should say. A short and quite small nose with fine nostrils. A pair of tight lips with long canines protruding between them. A very lean but muscular body covered in a fine duvet of fur (no colours are given here). My spine seems a little different but not really sure in what. And one final detail is really visible, my hands and feet have claws, not nails. Considering the number of injections they gave us so far, I'm really quite surprised to see just how little effect it truly had on our bodies meaning that, none of them really did anything yet. We will be injected again with all our previous choices plus the ten or so new ones and then a load of other things that depends on our group.

I choose to go down the same path as what I've been in so far, all the species of fox that they have, a few variants of wolves and then quite a bit of the feline realm. I go for panther and tiger to join Jenny in that, add in some leopard for the speed and then a bunch of other things that look cool like 'better breathing,' 'fast healing' and so on. When all of them are correctly selected, it pops out a list that reflects the final number of injections, I'll be getting that evening: 132. That's the moment when you want to hit the back button and deselect half of my choices but nope, can't do that. I'll just have to patiently wait out the moment when they are going to stuff all those needles into my spine and other soft tissues.

I think, for the first time since I got here, we were actually left to rest a little today. After we did all our choices of DNAs to be injected with and got the number spat in our faces, they thought we might want to get mentally ready to receive the injections. Jenny is getting 124, Amber 153, Hollie 92 and Saphyr is going to suffer most of all of us, she is getting just under 200. I asked her why and she simply said that she chose an entire drop-down menu as she could not choose. I think that's a mistake she will not make again. I mean, we end up passing out from the sheer amount of pain but it's still a little crazy to think that all those needles are going to be stuck into us.

Our rest period lasted quite a while and night has fallen outside for a while now. When they call out our group, 'Decembers, head to door 3 on the left side, go undressed!' we strip and head to our doom. Yeah, clothes are really not a thing here, they keep the place at a comfortable temperature all the time and thus expect us to see dressing as a luxury that we don't need.

I find myself holding hands with Jenny and Amber, Hollie and Saphyr holding theirs, as we walk single file towards the door. We are way too worried about what truly happens behind that door. The October group did not come back for an entire week when they went. We walk through the door to find a table with leather strips on it, each one engraved with a number, so I pick up 503 and then walk into the room. It looks a lot like a dorm but the beds are in circles of 7, heads all facing inward. We are told to take whichever we like and to lie on our stomachs. To my surprise, this order is actually given somewhat nicely, no please or thank you but a bit of softness. That actually scares me more, it means they are feeling a little pity for the pain we are about to endure. My circle ends up being with the girls and Rudolph and another girl from the group called Lena. We are all glancing around wondering how bad this is actually going to be.

Worst question ever!

Just as I look at Jenny and Amber, I see the white coats walk in and in their hands the cases. They start off by adding letters to our tattoos, mine thus becomes 'YC503-FWTL-D-FPLR-M.' Under that, they add a line and a set of digits in hexadecimal: 00132A, a colour code, a dark tint of blue. No idea why they put that there, probably as a joke. I don't really have time to question it, the strip of leather I picked up is pushed between my teeth and we are simply told to 'bite down'. The following moment I can remember is an explosion of pain like nothing I've ever felt, definitely worse than the first ones. I feel the needles from the base of my back going into my spine and up quite a way, a second one is put in where that one stops and a third and a fourth until they reach my neck. Then I start to feel the injection go in, the needle is removed and another takes its place. The pain does not cease and we are all crying out in pain and most of us faint from the pain rather fast.

Brief moments of consciousness flair with pain. More pain. Still more. At some point, I'm told to stand up but fall off the bed and puke up bile and probably blood. Next thing, I'm on my back and something shiny is way too close to my field of view. It comes closer and then the needle goes into my eye. I thought the ones in my back were bad that one is plain horrible. It feels like I would imagine acid and fire combined would be. I sadly don't pass out from that bit but I wish I had; the pain is totally unbearable but somehow my body doesn't want to help out. The needle is pulled out and then stuffed into my other eye. This time I finally pass out again but am quickly brought back to my senses with an incision being made into my arm and a muscle fibre being pulled out of it. Obviously, they did it on my right arm to not affect the tattooed area on the left.

Well, I passed out again, puked my guts out again and finally woke up in the dark, hearing grunts and cries of pain. I try to move but it's too painful and just makes me nauseous again.

To think that they would actually then go and stuff that piece of muscle back in and stitch it back. That last part was horrible, they had done something to it, dipped in something or I don't know what but it's been burning ever since. Every time I think of standing up my body just refuses and makes me want to hurl even more but there is nothing left. We are all starving hungry but no one can move. They have not bothered checking on us or bringing any form of food, the only person we see is a janitor who takes out our waste. I can't really describe how unpleasant it was to figure out that our digestive system is at a standstill and that all our nutrients are coming intravenously.

I finally managed to move myself to the edge of my bunk and sit up today, Amber, Hollie and Jenny had already managed that, Saphyr is still in too much pain, though. Let's be real here, she did get nearly a full thousand injections. And yes, before you wonder dear reader, the amount of DNA injected each time is extremely small but because they need to apply it to all the major nerve centres of our bodies, it implies a lot of injections. More than a lot, a day's worth. The numbers the machine had pumped out seem to have had no link to the number of needles we would get but were rather linked to the total fluid content or something.

To Leave or Not to Leave

I've not bothered relating the six months that followed our huge set of injections, it was basically hell but that is now usual. The catalysis hardly felt like anything after all those injections. Now that we have finally reached the end of the month of May, we are to move out of the main hangar room. We are showering for our last time when the buzzer announces the arrival of a new group and nearly fifty youths walk in. I almost smile when I see the boys in the group staring at us, naked, walking across the room to our bunks. We are to stay undressed and walk towards the D door. I just hope they're not going to go about injecting us with more stuff. As a group, we walk towards the door when the buzzer goes again and we are called to go faster. 'DMay group head to your door.' One sentence but a whole lot of anticipation from us. After the last time we spent there, six months ago, we are all somewhat worried about what is waiting for us behind that door.

It opens, we walk in and as soon as everyone is in, the door closes behind us. A distinctive lock click is heard and the next thing we see is a row of beds in the middle of the room. Our codes are on them so I head to 503 and sit on the edge of it.

Not everyone has a bed, in fact, only 6 of us remain. They turned the light down so much now that I can hardly see anything. A white coat comes in and says: 'All of you without a bed, follow me, the others, lie down for bed.' As always, we just do as we are told and lie down. As the others shuffle out, I see Amber and Hollie leave as well as Thorin one of the guys in the group. We lie down and that's when I realise that the bed is bare, it's nothing but a plastic covered mattress and no cushion at all. They basically went from treating us like slightly human rats to just rats. Sleep comes easily after today's excessively hard 6 hours of sport. I'm just glad to see that Jenny and Saphyr are still in here with me even if I'm starting to think that means we are going to be stuck here forever.

I'm woke up not feeling rested at all but in a totally different place and coughing on something strange. The place feels wrong, totally wrong. I'm floating. It's not bad, it's just wrong. I was sleeping and now I'm floating in something thick and sticky, my head and arms are held at the surface by a floaty thing. I look around in the dark and glimpse other figures in here with me. There are five so we are all in here and all floating in place, this stuff is too thick to swim in but I still try and head towards the others. As I slowly near them, I see that they are also making their way towards each other and so we end up in a circle. No one knows how we got here. In fact, it's quite a strange phenomenon, how did they move us without us knowing?

'Do you guys think they gassed us or something?' Asks Saphyr. 'Probably, it's not like they have any respect for us anyway.' Replies Sybil, another girl from our group with whom I've never really spoken. 'What do you guys think this stuff is, it feels really strange?' Asks Jenny. 'It's a gel form catalyser XC503, and yes you were gassed and you're about to be gassed with another type of gas, more catalyser. Oh, and don't bother holding your breath.' Comes a voice from everywhere and nowhere at the same time. Just as it cuts off, a whistling sound announces the gas being pumped into the room. The air also feels a lot like the time when they injected more oxygen into the air and made the pressure higher.

The gas they are making us breath has no smell or taste but it is opaque in a way that it seems like fog. I'm actually surprised that it's so easy to breathe it while the air is in such high oxygen content. I breathe in and out normally as much as I can but it still feels as if it's a mistake. We look at each other and realise that this is going to last quite a while.

'What do you think they did with the others, I mean culling the herd is one thing but this is a little violent?' I ask. 'Either killed them or put them in another lab or maybe even released them. We aren't going to find out by the feel of it.' Replies Amber. She is the one that always had jokes to tell when we got depressed in the main residential area. Not so joyful this time. 'They were released after we removed a full year of memory. And no, you won't be following them as we can remove a maximum of a year. If you leave here within the next year, it will be as ash.' Comes the voice again. 'And you've still got three and a half hours in there. If you need to relieve yourselves, go towards the light.' And, with those words, a single light comes on in what seems to be a corner. 'Damned I've been keeping it in for ages, I'll be back.' Says Jenny and splosh swims off into the fog of gas.

'So, little rats, did any of you get interesting changes that you have not reported?' Asks an all too familiar voice. 'You're all failures again, aren't you? And to think that you are all nearly blacks this time. 503 and 507 are so dark your DNA's is full of animal but none of it is showing. Yes, that's what the bottom hex code is, it's your DNA attribution colour. You'll be spending five hours a week in here and all the rest of your time will be in a high-oxygen environment for the next three months. After that, we'll be doing the same amount of catalysis but with half as much oxygen as in normal air. And after that, I've still got loads of ideas to make your bodies manifest the animals you truly are.'

He cuts off and we just bob slightly in the liquid wondering if there will be more to his monologue. 'Great, so we get to have a sticky bath once a week and we might potentially die from oxygen deprivation in three months' time.' Says Jenny, joining us again. 'I doubt they would kill us all off in one shot but yeah you're right, they are sure trying. And I thought the injections were bad, fuck this is going to be constant pain.' Replies Saphyr. 'I suppose we'll have to try and look after each other for that time.' Says Amber. We all agree on that and I'm just hoping they will allow us to be helping each other, we weren't really allowed to previously.

When we are told to make our way to a green light, the air clearing up a little, we all end up going single file into a tight corridor. As we all stand in the corridor, an instruction comes: 'Protect your genitals if you wish to keep them.' My hands go down and the girls have an arm around their breasts and a hand covering their privates. The door to the pool closed and a rumble starts. The next thing is somewhere between painful and horrible: from both the back and the front a blade of water is hitting us and going upwards. They somehow have the pressure just right so that keeps us standing and yet it feels like it's cutting off our skin. The water falling off us is a horrible blackish colour but no time to think of that, the water is hitting most of us straight in the private parts and it hurts, even with our hands trying to protect us. That part is soon over as it goes higher and when it reaches our necks stopes. Then a powerful shower starts and we are told to scrub off any residue.

When the guards are finally satisfied with our cleanness, a door on the other end opens and we shuffle out into a corridor and then through a door on our right into our room. The corridor is white and has a sort of plastic or glass against all surfaces, our room has this too. I suppose that has something to do with the control of our atmosphere. Inside the room are six beds, linked together to form a large rectangle with six mattresses. There are pillows and blankets but no clothing to be seen anywhere. Against one wall I see gym equipment, I guess the hours of sport will continue. Another wall has a door and a sort of trapdoor with a table in front of it, probably for food. Last but not least, the third and furthest wall has a shower and toilet area. Obviously, everything is open just like in the hanger room and there are cameras in each corner. They are leaving us in constant observation but it would seem as though they don't plan on having a guard in here. I suppose that means it's fully locked so we can't really go out anyway.

It's going to be time to sleep soon seeing that it's dark outside but the trap opens with a slight hiss and six bowls come through, six spoons and a jug or steaming splosh. Then a voice comes through invisible speakers.

'DMay group, you are now six. You will be in this room for the next six months and are to look after it to your best capacity. You will not need to clean the room as it is a closed, air filtered space. Your daily time's table goes as follows: Wake up, shower, eat, sport, eat, shower, sleep. You may speak to each other, play, do whatever you like so long as you follow that list and do 5 hours of sport a day. The times will be announced each day, respect them or your roommates will be told to punish you how we see fit. If you refuse to comply with any of the above rules, we will drop you all with 10,000 volts. The entire room is conductive so don't try to get away. Now, eat and when you're done place the pitcher back in the trap and close it. You are to clean the bowls and keep them so each day. I'm Angie, you'll be hearing and seeing me pretty often, I'm in charge of your group. Bye.'

We sit down, share out the splosh and eat. For the first time in a year, they actually give us time to eat. 'Shower' comes a synthetic voice over the audio system. As we are used to eating fast and basically gulping down the food, we were left with quite enough time to chat a little even if, after an entire year here, we have very little to talk about. Saphyr is still the most interesting of all of us. Her parents sent her here as opposed to the rest of us who got here from personal choice. Jenny and I are the only orphans, though, Amber, Sybil and Annop all ran away from abusive homes to end up here.

We head to the showers and soon we are washing our bowls and then ourselves. The tradition of 'you wash my back and I'll wash yours' has not changed. We then dry off with a stream of hot air and have free time, or it would seem. We head over to the large bed thing in the middle of the room, randomly claim a bed each (they did not number them this time) and sit on them. Before long we are all sitting on the three middle beds, the ones claimed by Annop, Jenny and Saphyr.

'Sleep!'

Life within the room

Although it started off in a slightly interesting way, the first few days we would wake up on about three and a half beds, all sleeping in a haphazard pile. We woke up laughing when the call for 'Eat!' came. But, now that this has been going on for nearly three months, we are trying to respect each other's space. Or at least I'm trying to. The girls and Annop often go to sleep hugging or holding hands. The food quantities are always the same, the times seem to be the same and sport is still as tiring. So, beyond the fact that we are rats in a lab and being constantly observed, the part that makes this all worse is that, whenever one of us isn't satisfactory to the overseers, then a single command comes 'Punish!' We have to then hit that person once each. I don't know if it's to make us hate each other or what, but we did not do it the first time only. Those 10,000 volts are not a joke, I was doing bench lifting and I ended up dropping the bar on my ribs. I have two huge purple bruises, even now, two weeks later.

The punish command happens twice to three times a week and has happened to me three times now. I just asked the others to do as they are told and hit me once each. The only problem with that is the amount of muscle we all have. I not sure what muscles and genetics have to do with each other, according to them, but they sure made us into lean monsters. To think that the first punch in the shoulder would knock me over was not expected but it became worse when the guards considered it was taking too long and gave a quick zap to everyone.

At some point, a white coat comes into the room, tells me to lie down on the bed and injects me with something into both the bruises. The pain numbs, he pulls out a scalpel, cuts me open right there and takes a look inside my chest. 'You have six broken ribs 503. I'll set them back and pin them in a minute.' He says pulling out tweezers and a bunch of other stuff. '502, come give me hand.' Jenny comes over and he tells her to use the tweezers to play puzzle with my bones and put all the bits back into place. The breaks are not clean. Apparently, I'm to be happy my lungs are not punctured. The next bit I would rather not retell in too many details; essentially the doc puts some sort of patty on my bones, stitches me closed and tells me to go wash the blood off. When the hot water touches the fresh stitches, I can't keep back bitter tears of pain. That shit burns like hell and we are to go catalyst swimming tomorrow.

The swims mark the week's passing, the pain and bruising of my ribs never fully subsides but it's now just a minimal irritation. The washing off from the catalyst bath is probably the thing we hate most at this point. It hurts like a mule kicking you no matter what you do. Yet, the thing we are all worried about is the upcoming change from the high oxygen air to the exact opposite. That is supposed to happen tonight at some time.

Well, great, we got woke up by a lovely electric shock and missed our morning shower. The change in air pressure and oxygen content was so that we are all gasping for air just to breathe. It made us pass out in our sleep and now we have to get up, go eat and do our hours of sport in this extenuated state. If experience is anything to tell by, we are going to be hitting each other every day for the next months and then probably getting zapped even more. I'm really starting to wonder if there is not a way we can get away from the 'punish!' command.

Thoughts and Acts of Leaving

Three months of low oxygen was hell, we were always tired, always depressed and worst of all, always getting 'punish!' as no one could finish the requested tasks in time. They now have us draw each other's blood once every two weeks and the first two attempts we ended up hurting each other quite a lot. It's not specifically hard to draw someone's blood with a syringe and it becomes easier with time but they were doing everything for us to fail in the task. Between giving us only one needle for everyone, no needle and telling us to use our teeth and even other crazy things like a knife. You may think that is horrible, they also have not given us any form of cloths ever again so we are naked at all times.

After they played with our air supply, they started playing with our food supply. Sometimes, a lot of food would come and we were to eat it all or we would have to punish each other. Sometimes, they would not feed us for multiple day and night cycles. This starts to seriously bring us down and not only that, it rapidly makes us sick. When we were all puking bile and feeling horrible, they started sending in smoothies and actual nice things as if to be forgiven; or maybe because they don't actually want to kill us all off.

After a few more weeks, we get given pencils and pens and we are told to write a weekly report on our physical status. The fact that none of us had written anything for more than a year and a half is one thing. The fact that none of us has anything to talk about is another. We get told to hit each other every time it takes more than a few minutes for us to write a full page of bullshit.

Two weeks after they started sending in the paper, one page came in with a drawing and a code, A1 and five lines. We discreetly copied it and made sure to try and figure it out. Following that one, A2, A3, A4 and everything up to D4 comes. When the lights turn off that night and go into night glow, we copy it over onto one of our backs. As soon as we have it all down, the meaning is obvious: it's a floor plan of the building. In other words, someone here is actually trying to help us out, or it's just another test to see if we can figure it out. We go to sleep but I'm sure that most of us are still awake in silence, trying to figure out what this floor plan can actually do for us.

The next day, during the only time we had where we could speak, we came to a rapid consensus, one of us would have to try and make it out to get help. With my luck, I drew the short straw and was selected to be the first one to try and make it out. I had no desire to leave Jenny behind but what choice do I have…

Three days of planning, of preparing everything, was all I got as, on the fourth day when the notes came, there was a line of writing: this is a key card. It is written on the back of the one notepad and that means I needed to take that piece without being seen on the cameras. As we are all forced to be naked, it's nearly impossible to hide anything but that excludes long hair. As we are not obligated to do so, most of us have long hair because we don't cut it. I thus hide the card by tying my hair down and sliding it under my thick curls. It's not the best hiding place but that's all I have and as I was chosen, it's my job. With that done, our reports are written and the papers sent away again, I just wait for any form of signal. We don't even know what time it is outside or if our day cycles are vaguely accurate.

With the help of the entire group: Amber, Hollie, Saphyr, Jenny and Anoop, I manage to get everything memorised and, on our next notepad, a message comes saying, 'Power outage in 30 minutes, you will be met by another person from the J group. Be ready.' That's strange, I did not think that whoever is helping us would give us that much information and I was even less expecting that I would not be alone. It does mean that we are going to be all the more visible and that we are going to have to figure food out and so on for more than one person.

That power cut comes so fast that it takes us by surprise, the door clicks open and there is a hiss as the air regularises. That's my call to go out, I give Jenny a hug and run for the door. Right behind it, two guards are waiting for me and they both yell at me to run faster while they throw me a sort of cloak-dress-thing. I run down towards the exit signs until I find a door to burst through. Outside, a girl is running ahead of me in the moonlight, I accelerate to catch up with her and immediately see that she is wearing the same sort of garment as myself and that she is also barefoot.

'Hey, wait up, we are already nearly a kilometre away.' I call out to her, but to no avail, she just runs on ahead so I try to catch up but she is surprisingly fast for someone who has lived through Cross-Gen for what must have been two years.

We continue running, cutting our feet on stones and low branches, falling and getting up in a hurry. Just as I thought we were finally far enough, the noise of 4x4s starts getting louder. It's going to be a pain to get out of here by the seeing of it. The girl stops. Turns around. Looks at me and say: 'We need to hide or run faster, either or, but we don't want to get caught.' I look at her and hope for more but she is waiting for me to respond. 'I think we need to run.'

I've no idea how long we run only that, when we stop, my feet are bleeding and so are my legs. I'm in pain and sweating. The girl fell over into a pile of straw in a field we were running through. I walk up to her and find her lying naked tearing bits of her cloak thing and strapping her legs and feet as they are bleeding. 'Hey are you going to strap yours or do you need me to do it for you?' she asks me. I sit next to her, take off my cloak thing and start strapping my feet first. 'I'll manage, thanks for asking. What's your name by the way? I'm 503.' I say totally forgetting that I actually have a name, not just a number. '523, nice to meet you 503. I think we should get going again soon, we are going to need to get more distance between us and them before we can think of sleeping and some clothes may be a good idea.' She says standing up and putting what's left of the cloak around herself again. It barely covers her and we are obviously going to need more than this to sleep in this cold night. If my maths is correct, it should be October right now but I'm not actually sure. 'What month do you think it is?' I ask 523. 'No idea, probably mid-autumn considering the leaves colour and fall.'

We continue on our way for quite some time, through sunrise and even more after that, but at a much slower pace as our feet are causing a lot of pain and bleeding still. Passing through towns is not easy so we stick to the fields and only go past the back of one shopping centre to see if we can salvage anything. 523 finds herself a pair of torn pants and a shirt and she finds me a dirty pair of jeans. We don't change immediately but take the stuff with us and wash them in the next bed of water we find. During that time, I try to get 523 to tell me a bit about how their group was treated but she is tired of the running and doesn't want to say much. I do find out what her name is: Byeol-I. It's Korean for 'star', I tell her my name, Haiylen.

Finally, dressed a little warmer, we continue on our way hoping for the best, heading dead south for now. Neither of us has a place to go but I want to head back to the orphanage and get my stuff there before I figure out my next step. Byeol-I was abandoned by her parents in Korea and Cross-Gen flew her here, to France, so she doesn't have any place to go. As we are now no longer running, we finally start talking to each other. Let me describe her to you. Bear in mind that we look nothing like we usually would as we have no body hair and we are dead tired, lean and aggressively muscular. She has long straight black hair. Dark brown eyes slanted slightly down on the edges and quite flat towards the nose. Her nose is fine and small, exactly like most of her other features. Her lips are fine and a deep red, her jaw slightly angular but fine and drawn. The rest of her is a little hard to describe with more words than that, she is lean, muscular, well drawn and fine. Her female attributes are not specifically marked but then neither is my male ones. We both believe that Cross-Gen must have something to do with this. She also speaks English with a Korean accent but it's good.

Making It Back

Three days of walking and only then do we feel safe enough to hitch a ride on the one road. The guy who picks us up speaks only French and is a total hippy. Thankfully, he doesn't ask any questions about our attire but does wink at me repeatedly for some reason. Conveniently, he is actually going almost all the way to where we need to go and, after chatting with us for nearly two hours he randomly offers to invite us over for the night and to drop us off the next day. We have not mentioned anything about the Cross-Gen stuff but I'm sure he figured out that there is something up. Teens don't usually walk around in battered cloths and have serial numbers tattooed on their arms.

He ends up asking us about our recent past when we are at his place, a little house in a town not far from our final destination. We are just outside of Brignoles so really not far from the orphanage, which helps a lot already, and we are quite a long way away from the Cross-Gen Centre. I give him just a tiny bit of information and before I say too much he says, 'don't tell me any more, I don't want you to feel uncomfortable for no reason. I'll take you to your old orphanage tomorrow and wait for you as you get your stuff. Then back here and I'll help you figure some stuff out, especially seeing that neither of you two have identity documents or a place to go.' It sounds too good to be true and I'm sure he knows because the first thing he says after that is 'but if you are worried to trust me, I can just drop you off there'. We ask him for the night to think it over and he says that we'll have to leave early as he needs to go to work in the afternoon. Aurel, by his name, shows us to the guest room and gives us some clothes to wear. Nothing fancy but a pair of sweat pants and a tee-shirt each. He didn't have underwear for Byeol-I but she said she doesn't mind; we have not worn any for two years and I go without as well.

The shower is amazing, the food was cool but this is just bliss. Byeol-I came with me and, as I would do with my group, we help each other clean fast. Less than three minutes to have everything clean and ready to dry off. We were never allowed more than three minutes of water at the centre. Neither of us cares even the slightest about nakedness, that has not changed. The short duration of the shower did not prevent soap from hurting our raw feet and legs but that was a small price to pay for the comfort of the shower itself. Aurel did not say anything when we got back to the lounge clean and dressed in the too big, borrowed clothes. We bid each other good night and head off to the rooms. A pleasure-full surprise, the guest room only has one bed and it is truly comfortable! We close the door, get undressed, hop into bed and pretty much just crash.

The next morning comes and, for the first time since I can remember, I feel rested rather than half dead. It actually takes a few slight shakes to wake Byeol-I up. We get dressed in our borrowed cloth and go out into the lounge to find Aurel waiting for us with what smells suspiciously like warm bread.

— 'I thought you two might appreciate some real food for the first time in a while, so I got my favourite bread from the local bakery to share on the road. Coffee is ready too so I'll put some of that into a flask and we can be off.

— Thanks so much for everything Aurel, that was the best night I've had since I can remember.

— Damn, and that's not even a good bed, if I'm being honest. You should really write a book about what was happening there one day and I'll read it.

— If I'm alive long enough to do that, I promise I will. Do you mind if I grab a coffee now, I've no idea what it even tastes like?

— Sure, and if Byeol-I wants some too feel free, I just don't want to delay anything in case you want to come back after.'

I ask Byeol-I and she says yes for the coffee but asks for sugar in it, a lot of sugar. I drink up quite fast even if the taste is super bitter, so I add sugar to mine too. Soon after, we are on our way towards the outlying village of Cuers, it's just over forty minutes' drive so we end up just chatting about Cross-Gen and listening to the radio. I asked Aurel if we could listen out in case there is a search going on for us but it would seem there is not. I mean, Cross-Gen can't be anything more than an illegal company. After all, playing with human genetics is forbidden under international law so they probably don't have a lot of licit power. We make it to the orphanage quite early and with no troubles whatsoever. I ask Aurel if he would mind waiting for me for ten minutes and thus give me enough time to find Mad and talk to her about getting my passport and so on.

As I get out of the car, Aurel stops it, climbs out and so does Byeol-I.

— Did you really think we were just going to let you walk into what could well be a trap? I mean seriously, you should be smarter than this 503! What if they are waiting for you here? Asks Star.

— And even if they are not, you may need someone to help get what you want from the matron, she doesn't seem like someone who just gives. Says Aurel.

— I didn't want to drag either of you into this and I also don't think she would have kept anything, I mean I never saw the cash that was found when they found me, she took all of that as well as anything personal to me.

— Let's just go, shall we?

We knock on the door and low and behold, Mad opens up almost instantly. She starts by asking who we are and what we want in a very polite tone and I don't have time answer before Aurel does. 'We are here to gather all the personal belongings of Haiylen one of the orphans here.' I can't actually believe she hasn't recognised me but, then again, I have very long hair now and I'm wearing newish clothes.

— 'What business do you have with him? His stuff was thrown out long ago as he ran away never to be found again.' Asks Mad in an annoyed voice.

— 'I'm pretty sure you never threw out that wad of cash or the box you could never open or anything else of his actually.' Aurel replies casually recounting details I told him during the drive here.

— 'I have no idea what you are talking about so please be on your way.' Replies Mad, casually closing the door in our faces. I don't let her, put my hand against it and slam it open.

— 'Of course you know what he is talking about you old cow, now get the key to the damned storage and let me get my stuff so I can be out of here and not waste the people's time longer than needed!' I say in a flat tone, trying to not sounds annoyed.

— 'Who the hell do you think you are to talk to me like that? I don't even know you, how do you have so many details. The guys three days ago knew nothing of the sort, they just want me to call them should he get back here. Where is that little shit and why do you know him, you better hand him over to the guys from the police.' She says looking both annoyed and overwhelmed, good for her.

— 'I'm standing right in front of you, I know your eyes suck but this is insane. Now let me get my stuff, please.' Stress on the, please.

She looks abashed and doesn't move for a while before saying that she is going to have to call the police. I look at her, smile and barge into the hallway. She didn't lock her office to come and open the main door so, I just casually walk in and grab the key chain off the wall and walk up to the second floor. I know where the storage closet is and, as I walk up towards it, I hear a huge clamour from downstairs and then Byeol-I shout up the stairs that I need to hurry. After that, all the current orphans here run up to the second floor and wait impatiently as I try the keys until I find the correct one and open the storage closet. The metal cube box I was looking for is sitting in the middle of the room, the only thing not slightly dusty. It has marks all over it from her trying to open it and failing. No idea what it's made of but it's certainly strong. I don't think my passport would be here, it's probably in the office, so I leave the other residents so that they can raid the storage to their heart's content. A few of them know who I am and say 'Hi' but not much more. As I head down to the office, I hear Mad is still yelling incomprehensibly.

When I get down the stairs, I hear Aurel talking to Byeol-I saying that we need to get out of here as Mad has called Cross-Gen. The business card sitting on her desk with the phone number highlighted it from there. Byeol-I is holding my passport, somehow having found it, and smiling at me. Mad sees me with the box and just says, 'You'll never get it open, it's unbreakable.' I don't know why but I have a feeling that I'll be able to open it anyway. I mean, if it was left there for me, chances are I can open it somehow. We walk out the front door with Mad tailing behind and trying to keep us in while the Cross-Gen people get here but Aurel pushes her out the way. We make it to Aurel's car but, by the time he gets the engine started, there are screeching tyres in the little parking lot as the guys from Cross-Gen appear. The leave their engines running and jump out. Aurel slams the accelerator and thankfully he is good at driving. He gets us going towards the road but not fast enough to avoid a few bullets being shot through the windows. He is missed but one bullet graze my shoulder pretty deeply and shattered glass peppers all of us. Byeol-I gets hit in the shoulder but through the seat so it's not deep. We are both so used to pain and covered in scars from all the Cross-Gen stuff but it's uncomfortable nonetheless. We get to the village and then head straight to the nearest police station for security.

We get to their parking lot and immediately realise it was a bad idea, two SUVs, exactly like the ones who were at the orphanage are parked there. Aurel drives on but not before taking pictures of the number plates on those two vehicles.

— 'I'll get us to the nearest city but I don't have enough fuel to go further. I'm glad I was there to drive you away; they would have killed both of you.' Says Aurel.
— 'And I feel bad for putting you in this situation.' I reply.
— 'Well, I could have not picked you up that day, I've got little to nothing to lose so you know, this is actually quite fun although it's risky.' He affirms.
— 'You're really nice.' Says Byeol-I.

We drive on, at a little over the speed limit, and make it to the city but we are clearly being followed and soon caught up. No way to get to the police station in time to get away from these guys and that is going to be a problem. As we round a corner, a red light stops us and a ton of traffic prevent us from even trying to go forth. The SUV comes up beside and behind us and, next thing we know, tinted windows are going down and guns coming out. Aurel tells us to duck just as he hits the accelerator. It's sadly not fast enough to save us completely. Byeol-I gets shot in the leg, Aurel in the arm and me in the shoulder. How he manages to drive in this situation must be pure adrenaline.

That Aurel gets us to the police station is the first miracle that none of us died yet is a second one. As he stops the car, three police men come out and help us out of the car. They don't ask any questions but get us inside the station and take us to a little infirmary. A bullet gets pulled out of my shoulder; I did not even know it was in there. It hurts a lot but it's still not as bad as the injections. As the nurse looks after us, we hear a huge amount of noise from outside and, apparently, it's guys from Cross-Gen shooting up Aurel's car. We are told not to move, not that we were going to, and soon screeching tyres and a lot of angry shouts can be heard.

It takes a while for things to calm down and when they do, a lot of angry voices can be heard behind the door, then an explosion.

That was loud, very loud.

'Who the fuck are these guys?' Asks a police woman running into the room. 'They just blew up your car and nearly killed three of my colleagues.' She looks at us for answers but we can't really answer without saying things that could be a problem. 'You're going to need to talk, they are gone, we'll come and interrogate you in a minute, don't move!' She says and walks out, fulminating.

A few minutes later, they called an ambulance and decided to move all of us wounded people to the hospital. It only takes a few minutes to get there and when we do it's a question of stitches and angry voices until all wounded parties are patched up. Then, they drive us back to the station and into an interrogation room, with an interpreter for Byeol-I and then it starts.

— 'Let's start with you Mr Cavelier, can you start from the beginning of your encounter with these two.' Asks the police investigator to which Aurel responds by recounting all the events that brought us to meet.
— 'So, if I understand correctly, you helped these two renegade-looking teens out of selflessness, put yourself in harm's way to help them and even took a bullet for strangers?' Asks another inspector.
— 'That's correct officer, I do think you need their back story too, though.' Replies Aurel.

— 'Yes, please do tell us more Mr Glass and Mrs Shyn.'

I go through the process of explaining everything from being found in the port to running away from Cross-Gen. At some point they stop us and bring in food and water. When I'm done, they ask to see the injection scars on both of us so that they can photograph them for the investigation. They also place us under protective custody until we are considered safe. As Byeol-I doesn't have identity documents, they have her fill out asylum paperwork. As for me, I'm considered French so there is little to nothing for me to do. Aurel missed work and thus has to deal with that but the police give him a very good alibi: terrorism. As his car was destroyed in a criminal way, his insurance will help and should also help for his work absences for a few days.

They move us to a hotel and we are requested to stay there, under fake names, until next Monday. No one questioned my strange and damaged metal box but I need to figure it out. Aurel is taken home after we are dropped off at the hotel and we move into our room. Thankfully, they even planned ahead and got us some comfortable track suit cloths as all we had burnt in the boot of the car. Byeol-I and I are given separate but linked rooms though we quickly tell them that 'for security purposes' we will only use one.

After taking one of the longest showers either of us have ever had, together, we sit down on the bed, naked as always, and start looking at the box and how to open it. There seems to be no cracks or any opening direction, up or down. The only hint is in the form of two dents on opposite sides of the cube that seem to have some use. Star tells me I should try putting my thumbs in them and see what that does. I do but nothing happens. I then try all my other fingers in pairs and then in various combinations but nothing happens.

   — 'Do you think it needs some form of power maybe?' Asks Byeol-i,
   — 'I don't know, maybe, but how would I give it power?
   — You have a point. I mean, the only other thing I can think of is to try your big toes even if that's a little absurd.
   — Yeah, it kind of is, but you never know how much of a comedian the person who made this.
   — Try it.'

I get my legs up and around the box and put my big toes against the two dips and just then, leaving both of us to pick up our dropped jaws, a little click is heard. We are both taken aback by the mechanism, but then again not that much; I'm pretty sure that if it was only my fingers, Mad would have opened it before. I lift the now split in half box and obviously it's upside down. The content falls out on the bed in the form of another box and a letter. I push the box aside and look at the letter, it's addressed to me 'Haiylen' and has a wax seal on the back of it. I crack it open and unfold the content.

'Pelko Haiylen, me'i zon, Ert li n'a lix ta, er l'aa gernid. Kri'sl'é t'uh fertaa 'n t'uh séèr. Kaer n'a ert plexss, n'uh atait t'uh.'

Followed by a village name in Scotland. Although the language is nothing normal, I somehow understand what it says. It's an invitation to return home written by my father and a sister I did not know I had.

— 'Well, that's awesome, you have a place to go and you can see your parents again.' Says Byeol-I in a somewhat sad voice.
— 'You do realise that if I can go home, I'll take you with me. We are in this together now. The only problem is going to be paperwork.
— You go first and then I'll come over when my paperwork is sorted out.
— I'm not leaving you behind, it would be stupid of me to do that, especially that the protective custody is only going to last so long.
— You should check the other box and see what's in there. It may well be worth your time. Who knows maybe it's a ton of cash.'

I look at the smaller box and find nothing on it other than a groove around the middle of it. I run my fingers around the grove and somehow manage to cut myself on it. The moment my blood drips onto the grove the box clicks open. 'How the heck does this thing even work, where did it get enough power to do a blood or DNA test and open itself like that?' is the first thing I want to ask but then I see what's inside as Byeol-I lifts the lid. It's got only one thing in it, a solid slab of gold.

— 'Well, that will solve the question of paying for a flight and definitely solve the paying for paperwork.
— I don't think you should fly; train is probably a safer option even if it's longer. You don't know where these people are looking.' Replies Byeol-I.
— 'You have a point, but first I'm going to need to convert this into cash. That's going to be complicated even if I have ID and an address.

The gold ingot is marked and certified by the Scottish Royal Bank and it even has its ownership certificates, in my name: 'Haiylen Glas'. As much as that is going to help, I'll still need to find a place ready to buy this off me in cash and then be able to justify it all to the police as we are still in protective custody and they are watching us at all times. It's time to sleep so we lie down on the bed, after having locked everything back into the box, and fall asleep facing opposite sides of the room, backs touching.

Outside

The challenge of bureaucracy and a fire

Monday came and I managed to negotiate with the officer looking after us so that he would do the transaction for me, from gold to cash, and I thus paid for the hotel and ordered us some stuff online after having been shown an awesome online shop called Amaze-on. I got us some clothing, a set of cheap cell phones with prepaid plans and I could even get us some knives for extra security. I had to get them following specifications after the police told us what the legislation is. Once everything gets here, we are also told that the emergency travel documents I asked about for Byeol-I are an option. I wanted to know if we would be able to get her paperwork to travel to Scotland with me and, apparently, it's possible. We request them and are told to book the train tickets as it will only take 24 hours to get the paperwork.

Nothing really happens for the three days before our train trip is supposed to depart. Although the documents are fast to acquire, there is a limited timeframe in which we can be accompanied for the trip. After a while, the police only do rounds rather than stay here all the time. We are simply told to stay safe and not bother the neighbours. Although it's not the best season, we go swimming every day and order all the nice food we can eat. Somehow, although you would think we would want to forget about it, we keep a lot of the Cross-Gen routines and do nearly 6 hours of sport every day. At one point, one of the police officers decided to join us but gave up after ten minutes saying that our routine is harder than special ops training. That is, of course, incomprehensible for either of us, we were not military trained, we were being tortured. I don't know what he meant but it bothers me to think that he may be right, maybe we were being trained as military. In most regards we have no idea what Cross-Gen's motives were.

Packing our bags takes very little time as we don't own much and thus it's all in cases within minutes. The police insisted on escorting us all the way to the channel tunnel and then handing us over to their counterparts from England. They don't take it lightly that our arrival at their station was so violent. Thus, we leave from the hotel with two undercover officers in an unmarked vehicle and make it to the train station with no hassles. However, as we get there, things get a little more complicated. Not only are there hundreds of migrants trying to get on the train without a ticket but also, I recognise three guards from Cross-Gen. We tell the police this and are immediately told to walk in a nonchalant way until we get to the train itself, at which point, they rush us into first class and then stay on guard. When the train finally leaves, more than a half hour late, we are told that the time to Paris is going to be three and a half hours. The two officers with us sit down and block us in so that we are not too visible and we then pull out a pack of cards. Rather awkwardly at first but soon becoming more comfortable with us, they are nice and teach us some games making time literally fly by. As much as the train is high speed, as in 350 km/h high speed, we are also having enough fun that it seems as though it's been 20 minutes when they announce our arrival in Paris.

Due to the distance between the station we arrive in and the one where the train to London leaves from, we have to commute through the centre of Paris and thus I ask if we could get out of the subway and look at some of the landmarks along the river Seine. We do exactly that, stopping at the 'Ile de la Cité' and to our great horror and astonishment, Notre Dame is on fire. The two officers with us bracket us in and, after only a few minutes of looking at the flames lick the side of the building, we are ushered along the river towards another landmark.

— 'Sorry guys, I can imagine you would have loved to look at that more but it's really too exposed and we are clearly being followed so I would like to avoid getting you in a crowded area.' Says Theo, one of the officers.

— 'That's fine, it's just sad to think that the only time I saw that beautiful cathedral was in flames. I think we better skip staying too long by the Eiffel Tower, I don't know how but I can smell Cross-Gen people following us.' Says Star.

— 'Yeah, we need to get to the train anyway, it leaves in two hours and I want to grab food.' Replies Damien, the other officer.

— 'Let's do that then. Tower, food, train.' I say as we get to the huge metal structure.

To go from the tower to the train station is a matter of minutes, we then hurry to get out of crowds and get food, everyone is rushing to the fire and thus away from the direction we are going. Once at the Eurostar station we look around for a place to eat and thankfully find one quite easily. Both Byeol-I and myself order red meat, for some reason we have been craving meat recently. It's almost as though the animal genetics in us are starting to actually do something…

If you are wondering, dear reader, why I am not spending much time on details in this relation, it is simply due to the lack of importance of said details to me. Now that it seems as though the meat has kicked up some form of animal instinct, I'd better start putting in much more detail. So, forgive me but here they come!

The meat just arrived on our beautiful oak wood table. The table has obviously seen many customers over years and years of usage, in some parts the wood is stained and even carved up by ambitious customers wanting to show their presence to the future patrons. Our plates are typical white porcelain but the meat on them, large T-Bone steaks is what really catches the eye. Not only does it barely fit on the plate, it is also so full of juice that it's dripping off onto the table. Star stuck hers with a knife and is slicing it into long strips. The two officers with us are eating far more healthy Caesar salad and are observing us young ones wolfing down these huge steaks. The restaurant is not specifically crowded and, to my great relief, the people from Cross-Gen, whom we think were following us, seem to have lost our trail.

We finish our food and head out into the train station again; it's noisy and crowded beyond any reason. There are so many people, smells and so much noise it's overwhelming. We rush to the train, walk down the platform with our luggage and it's immediately better. The two officers wish us well and tell us that they warned their English counterparts about the risk from the Cross-Gen private militia. We thank them for keeping us safe thus long and soon they leave us in the small four-seat cabin as the driver announces the train's departure.

It's a long, long way ... but to where?

It may come as no surprise that the ride to England was both fast and uneventful, yet strange in many ways. Star and I felt utterly suffocated for the entire time we were under the sea, almost as if our bodies knew exactly what was going on. When the train surfaced again and sped on to London, we were just relieved and actually feeling quite sick. Once the driver announced we were arriving in London, a member of the onboard staff came to us and told us to wait in our cabin as we were to be escorted. The train stopped and the frenzy of people wanting to get off started but not long after the noise began two large men came to our cabin. Us two travellers instinctively reacted and had our hands behind our backs on the hilt of our knives.

— 'Good day Haiylen and Star.' Says left dude smiling. 'Sorry love can't say your real name for the life of me.' He says to Byeol-I. 'Welcome to the UK, Theo and Sam told us to come get you so no need to stab us okay.' He said, still smiling.

— 'How can we be sure you are not Cross-Gen?!' I reply, on guard.

— 'Like this.' Right-dude pulls out a very official badge saying 'London Police' on it.

— 'Well, I hope that's not a fake one and I hope we can trust you.' I reply to him.

— 'You sure can kido, now let's get you two out of this train and onto the one north. I suppose you were not going to drive there, right?' Asks Lefty.

— 'Neither of us has a licence so train or hitching a ride it was to be.' I reply.

We get off the train framed by our two police blokes. Funny fact, a kid asked his mum if they are rugby players because they are, and I quote, 'huuuuuuggeeee.' They tell us getting a train up to York and then switching to one going to Glasgow is the easiest at this time of day but it will still take us nearly 6 hours to get there. We go get the tickets after exchanging our euros for sterling at the booth. At the booth they tell us that a direct train is bound to leave in 12 minutes and we can make it so that's what we end up taking rather than waiting an hour for the York train. Lefty and Righty don't say much but get us to the next train and then simply tell the staff onboard that we are to be checked up on often as we are in protective custody. They then call ahead to Glasgow and ask that we be escorted to a hotel upon arrival.

Only when the train is about to leave do I realise we will get to Scotland at 5 in the morning and thus we really need to sleep. Clothing is still uncomfortable to us but, as Star says, there are people around who would not understand. I take the first sleep shift as Star wants to look out the window for a bit. I lie with my head in her lap and fall asleep almost immediately. The train is slowing down when I wake up and

Byeol-I is fast asleep on me, so much for keeping watch. I get up slowly, trying not to move her too much and then the lights come on. 'Ladies and Gentlemen, we are arriving in Penrith station, please take all personal belongings with when leaving the train.' That means we are two stops away; we must have slept nearly four hours. I softly put Star's head onto my lap, hug her and promptly fall asleep again. The next time we both wake up together, we are being shaken awake by a tired-looking Scot.

— 'We just made it to Glasgow you two, I think this is where you are getting off. I overheard the officers talking when you got on, sorry.' He says.
— 'Thanks a lot for waking us up, I did not realise it's not the last stop of this train.' I reply trying not to show I'm on guard.
— 'No worries but you better dash, the stop is only for 5 minutes.' He says before going back to his seat after saying bye.

We run off the train, making sure we have all our stuff and barely make it off before the train starts moving again. On the platform, no one is waiting so we head into the station proper and then a bedraggled, sleep deprived, officer comes up to us and tells us that the London Police asked for us to be escorted to the nearest hotel. We get there on foot in less than three minutes, bid the officer goodnight and get a room. Before he leaves, the officer tells us to come by the police station the next day for clearing and then we can get to our final destination. Once in the room, we lock the door, strip naked as though our lives depended on it and run for the bathroom to get a shower. This is the first time in nearly 24 hours we have been free of garments and been able to get clean from all the travel grime. The Pavlovian nature of this is not the least ironic; we are running away from Cross-Gen but still act as they trained us. Cleaning is a wonderful feeling and we end up sitting back to back in the warm bath, nearly falling asleep. Just as I get out of the bath and help Byeol-I out too, she points out that I have a slight bump at the bottom of my spine. I definitely did not have that before.

— 'Do you think it's the hybrid thing starting to take effect?' She asks me.
— 'It's either that or I just hurt myself and, because of Cross-Gen, I may be too immune to pain.
— That's possible too, yeah. By the way, did you realise you're excited?' She asks smiling.

I don't understand for a split second and then realise that, for the first time in many years, my body has reacted to the presence of a naked girl next to me. Well, that was awkward but it did allow us to figure something out, they had put hormonal suppression drugs in our food at Cross-Gen and it took this long to wear off. Byeol-I then added that it was quite strange for none of the girls to have had their periods during the entire time and that, even though we were all naked no one ever got excited. In fact, we were so uninterested it's almost as though they suppressed even the natural human needs with those drugs. Obviously at 14 no one is specifically interested in that but come 16, and later 18, it's a different story.

We get a good night's sleep and, even with our newly recovered physical attraction, neither of us is bothered by the other's presence. We remain naked through breakfast in the room and then go to the gym for an hour before the police come to find us.

— 'Good mornin' you two, hope the night was good,' says the one officer. 'My name's Trevor and I will be in charge of you until you get to your destination. I have Star's asylum documents transferred from France to Scotland as you are now under our custody.' He goes on.
— 'Thank you, sir.' Says Byeol-I.
— 'No sir for me lass, just Trevor is fine. We'd better get going, though, that address is 2 hours drive away if the traffic is okay.' He says and turns tail. 'I'll wait for you in the lobby, get ready and we can go.' He adds.

We run up to our room, strip, shower at full speed and then get dressed again. Neither of us is fond of underwear but I think we don't have a choice this time. Back down in the lobby, Trevor finished a coffee and we grab some to go before heading to the carpark. We get into an unmarked car and are off immediately.

— 'If we make it through this little bit of traffic, it's clear open roads all way after.' Says Trevor.

— 'Silly question but, is there anything there where we are going?' I ask.

— 'Just the Rogue mansion but it's been locked down for a while, we all bet that you're the next inheritor and that's why you'd be able to get in.'

— 'Is Rogue a family name? Because, if so, I doubt I'll be able to, my surname is Glas, given to me at the orphanage.'

— 'That's not your birth name though I would think. There is a large bet back at the office that you will get in.' Oh, great, so they are even betting on this now. That's wonderful, not.

— 'I suppose we'll see when we get there.' I reply then looking out the window.

The drive takes a bit longer than planned and is both beautiful and boring. The scenery is really nice but the car rapidly became silent and then we put on the radio for the rest of the way. I can't actually believe what's happening, I may just find out about my birth family today and maybe even meet some distant relatives.

We arrive in a small town and I recognise the name as being on the address I found in the safe box. We are nearly there. Trevor drives straight through the town and turns off the main road at the end. Two more turns and we are stopped in front of a set of massive iron gates. They are attached to stone pillars and from either side of those a very tall fence with razor wire continues. Considering how remote this place is, it's surprisingly secure. There is nothing remarkable about what's behind the gates, just a winding drive with a thick forest on either side. No mansion is to be seen from here so I'm not really sure what they mean by that but the gates are intricate enough to announce something big. The two iron gates are made up of many interlacing animal shapes. In front of them, on the right-hand side is a small pillar with some sort of interphone on it. 'I would recommend you go call and we can see what happens from there.' Says Trevor.

I get out the car and go up to the intercom thing but I don't have time to press the call button that a voice is already talking. 'Welcome back Master Falawk, please wait for the shuttle to come get you. Your guests are permitted to come as well.' I don't understand but signal for the others to come out too. The gates open and a droplet shaped black vehicle arrives and opens for us to enter. Once its doors are closed and we are all three seated, it shoots off at a crazy speed through the trees and we are then at the foot of the famous mansion.

Rogue Mansion

When the droplet-shuttle stops, we get out and walk up to the door of the mansion. Let me tell you, it really deserves its name as a mansion. I count four floors and at least twelve windows per floor. The facade is just off-white and a large satellite dish is visible over the edge of the roof. The doors swing open silently as we walk up to them and thus, we end up in a quite unassuming small entryway. A single set of stairs leads off in the right and I can hear someone running down them at full speed. Before I have time to see much else, a pretty girl, I would reckon about 16 years old, long gold-brown hair flowing behind her as she runs, jumps straight into my arms and kisses me on the cheek for a full three seconds before hugging onto me.

— 'Leyna, could you let go of your brother before you suffocate him? Poor guy is going to be traumatised.' Says a middle-aged man appearing out of a side door in the hall.
— 'But Dad, you know I've been missing him all these year.' Says the girl, who is apparently my sister I did not know I had.
— 'You did not even welcome him home or say hi to officer Trevor or Byeol-I his travel companion.' Says the man to Leyna.

— 'So, welcome to Rogue HQ officer Trevor and Byeol-I. Welcome home son! He says to us. 'Follow me to the living room if you will.'

I don't know how to react between the appearance of a sister I was unaware of and a dad I can't seem to remember. It all seems so surreal I hardly want to believe it but Star comes up behind me and tells me 'You're not dreaming.'

Once in the lounge, a simple looking yet tastefully decorated room with a large wooden table in the centre, we sit down in a set of couches and the conversation goes on.

— 'Excuse me Mr Rogue, are you actually the real Dr Pieter Rogue from Genesis labs?' Asks Trevor.
— 'Yes, that's me and yes, I'm officially dead, I'll be getting that cleared up with the media and officials soon don't worry. Oh, and yes you won the bet, Haiylen is my son and thus has access to our house.' Says Mr Rogue, Dad, Pieter... I don't know what to call him.
— 'How do you know about the bet? We only spoke of that in the lounge with my colleagues.
— Yes, exactly, and my wife designed the security system you lot are running. I have a crawler running in the entire world tracking uses of the Rogue name. I still have many enemies out there.' Wait, what the hell did I just get myself into. I can see Leyna beaming at me from the other couch and I nod my head at her.

— 'You realise that's spying against your country which is illegal, right?

— You can't put a dead man in court and, by the time I'm officially alive again, it will be gone. I only did it to find out where my research has been used.' He looks a Trevor in a very matter-of-fact way. 'If you don't mind officer, I would like to talk to my son now and not just defend a stupid bet.'

That turned into an invitation to leave as my apparent little sister promptly dragged him to the door and kicked him out the house. From that moment on, it has been rather awkward as I don't know what to say to my dad whom I don't even know, or my sister for that matter. The next thing that happened was that, after Trevor was gone, Dad asked if we need food and both of us travellers said yes. I don't know how the heck they manage to do shopping if he is supposed to be dead and I also don't understand how I have a younger sister if I never met her. I thought I was found when I was around 8 years old so it's rather hard to understand. It's only around the dinner table that we finally start to get some form of explanations, but it seems like my 'dad' still has a hard time being fully open about things but I get the gist of it.

— 'Wait a second, you literally messed with the mind of an eight-year-old to block memories of his childhood. That's kind of fucked up you know?' What a lovely topic to bring up.

— 'You were 9 actually and yes that makes you a legal adult now as you are 18. It was that or this entire process would never have worked out. I needed to make sure you would be a blank slate so I made sure the amnesia was real. It can be reversed, though.' Seriously, what the hell, why was that not the first thing he said.

— 'For all I know you're going to mess it up even more but, if you can swear to me that it's going to work, I really wonder why you didn't do that immediately.

— You need to be fully rested for one thing and secondly, as much as I trust you, I need you to trust me.' That's not scary at all 'dad', not at all.

The subjects of conversation kind of stop after that, I don't really know what to think of all of this so I just ask for a shower. I kind of got used to the fact that my body hair is growing back now but I still want to be clean at all times. I guess it's a textbook case of Pavlov's dog, it's hard to get out of a habit once you have been formatted into it for so long. My sister, whom I must say looks a lot like I remember my mother, because yes somehow that memory flared up when I saw her, tells me that we can follow her up to our suite. I can't actually believe how huge this house is, two floors up and there are still two more plus a basement and the corridors seem endless and they have others splitting off of them in various places too. Leyna takes us to a double door and opens that, behind it is a short corridor with three doors, one left, one right and one at the end.

— 'Bathroom is at the end and you can choose to sleep in the same room or either of you can have mine. I'm on the right.' She says.

— 'I don't really know what to say, mind if we get clean before choosing?' Asks Byeoli-I.

— 'Sure, do you guys want to go together? It's way big enough even I could join you.

— That sounds like a plan, then we can talk a bit without Dad around.' Damned I have a hard time calling him dad.

— 'Oki doki, let me get you both some clothing. Byeol-I, mind wearing some of my stuff? I think it will fit. We will order clothes and stuff for both of you tomorrow.

— Sure, that's fine as long as you don't mind sharing, and as long as you have stuff my size, I'm a little bigger than you.

— Nah, I got you! And yeah, I have a bunch of fun too big stuff that will fit you.'

Right after that, she runs off into her room, then into what is to be our room and comes back with everything we need. I totally forgot that we actually have stuff but, in her rush to help us, I'll rather let her do her thing and be a kind host. We head into the bathroom and I immediately understand why she said we would all fit in here. The bathroom has a double Japanese bath system, one steaming hot and the other far more tempered. There are showers against the one wall and two doors off to one side that I guess are the toilets. Before I have time to say anything, Leyna throws five bath bombs into the hot bath and immediately the room fills with bubbles. She then turns something on that makes the baths turn into a jacuzzi like thing and the room immediately steams up.

— 'I don't know about you guys but this makes me a little more comfortable.' Says Leyna.

— 'What do you mean?' Asks Byeol-I.

— 'I've never been naked around anyone since I was old enough to clean myself.

— Oh, we were not dressed for the past two years pretty much all the time; Cross-Gen didn't exactly care about us and what the heck are genders anyway. I don't think puberty ever hit any of us properly.' Says Byeol-I pointing out something that I was thinking but did not put into words.

— 'You guys should let dad do some blood work, they probably messed with your hormones in some way. I would know, I've been studying those things since I was 10. Yeah, that's young but it is true, I graduated from high school at 9 through an online system.' The way she just says that is almost funny but it does remind me of myself and the fact that I should have graduated years earlier than I did.

— 'Waou, that's early! Damned you two are both super smart, aren't you!?' Says Byeol-I sounding rather surprised.

— 'Does Dad have the needed materials to do blood work here or does it require an external lab?' I mean it's not exactly like I am looking forward to knowing but it would be rather interesting if he has all of that.

— 'Oh yeah, the entire third and fourth floors are labs, and the top floor is a huge testing area. We even have a small shooting range outside. Dad is big on teaching me to defend myself and I'm pretty sure he is going to be the same with both of you two. That is if Byeol-I is going to stay with us.' Yeah, that's the next question, do we look for her parents now? I mean I guess so.

— 'I can't really remember the address of the house, I think two years of Cross-Gen ended up messing with some of my memory but I would like to go home, that's for sure. After all, I have travel papers now.' She says back, half sniffling. I can somehow see perfectly fine in this steamy room but I have been trying not to, I want to respect my little sister's wish for privacy.

Our conversation and bath continue on for a while and, once we are done getting every last part of our bodies clean and then dry, we retreat to Leyna's room to continue our discussion. I don't when exactly but at some point Byeol-I falls asleep against my back, lying on my sister's bed. I'm starting to get used to thinking of Leyna as being my sister. There are simply too many things about her that I recognise as being similar to me and she even has a birthmark that I somehow remember my mother having. One of the only memories I seem to have gained access too since getting here and seeing my sister. I have no idea how long we spoke but the sun was rising by the time Leyna fell asleep, her head on my chest and I followed into sleep seconds later.

We woke up long after I would have thought, it's currently 11:30 and we are all three headed down to lunch. Dad is waiting for us with a table full of food and loud 80s rock music playing. He seems so happy to see us that it's actually kind of scary. He greats Leyna with a huge hug and then kind of half hugs Byeol-I and me. We sit down and, somewhat unexpectedly, Dad and Leyna hold hands and offer theirs to Star and myself. I take my dad's hand and close the circle with Byeol-I and then we pray. After being in a Catholic orphanage for so long, this shouldn't surprise me in the slightest yet it somewhat does. Dad is a scientist and yet believes, that's a rather strange combination.

We talk about so many things that I almost get lost but the biggest subject, the elephant in the room, is Cross-Gen. After a while dad brings it up and asks us if we want him to do anything for us. I don't really understand so I ask what he means and his answer is so straightforward that it freaks me out.

—   'I created the cross-genesis processes with your mother, that's why they tried to assassinate us the day of that accident you remember.' Wait. What? How is that even possible? I don't really know what to say but the answer comes in the form of a question.

— 'Can I get my memory back?'

I don't know why but I have a feeling that I'll understand a lot more about all of this once I can at least remember my childhood. He smiles at me and asks me to follow him upstairs right after asking the girls if they would mind clearing up the dishes. Although my trust is running rather thin, I follow my dad to the third floor. Down one corridor, turn right, down another and into a lab. Strangely, the place looks as though there are usually many people working here; it's as if he had a huge staff at some point.

He has me lie down on an MRI table and then puts a bunch of ceramic like electrodes on my head. He also asks me for an arm so that he can take a vial of blood for genetic testing. I half-heartedly gave him my arm, I'm kind of sick and tired of needles but at least he took blood from one of the scared-up holes so I hardly feel a thing. I could see the slight cringe when he saw my serial code tattoo but he said nothing. The next step is my memory reboot. He asks if I want to be put under for that but I refuse. It's not that I want to appear tough or anything to do with my new pain resistance, nothing can be as bad as the spinal injections, I just want to know what he is doing to me. He warns me that the mental unlock will sting and then hits a few keys on a control pad and I let out a slight growl of pain. It feels like my head is going to explode. I hear my sister and Stary burst into the lab but then I black out.

Results and so many questions

I woke up from my blackout only a few minutes later but by then Byeol-I had given a vial of blood to Dad and he had run tests on our blood results.

— 'This is going to be rather difficult to explain kids, according to your blood tests, only my son's blood has active animal DNA. Byeol-I you have it there but it's basically dormant.

— What does that mean dad? I don't feel anything different in my body and I haven't seen any strange signs.' It's not that I don't believe it, but the idea that what Cross-Gen did actually works has me rather taken aback.

— 'Simply put, although it's hardly doing anything, your body seems to be accepting the foreign DNA, something which the cross-genesis has never seen before. Your late mother and I had both tried cross-genesis on ourselves and nothing worked. My current hypothesis is that the presence of our altered DNA in you may be the reason why you have it active. I did also find that they were using a lot of hormonal disruptors and thus neither of you two have really hit puberty. Well – you did in regards to age but not biology – especially you Falawk, you have a lot of contradicting hormones it's strange.

— Okay wait what? You and my mother were messing with your genetics? Is that not rather stupid?

— Well, it's not messing when between the two of us we had seven PhDs in genetics and bioengineering. And yes, we did but nothing ever worked and this was when our lab was funded by the army.

— Oh well that's reassuring, not.' I can't believe they would do that to themselves even if they knew exactly what they were doing. 'I suppose I need to get used to you being a mad scientist, huh? And when are my memories actually going to come back?

— Give it three days, I'll run more tests on your blood and figure out what hormones they killed off so that you can supplement them and activate your puberty to get your body back to a more natural state.'

We go over many different options and then, as time had moved on a lot faster than I thought, we head back down to one of the rooms on the first floor and, sitting in front of a bank of computers, we start looking for all the things we could possibly need. One of the first items I want is to get books but Leyna tells me that all the books I want to get are already in the house. I need to catch up to her and dad in sciences so that I can understand what Cross-Gen actually did to us, especially if it's going to affect me in some way. I am utterly clueless on what could possibly happen. A part of me doesn't really want to know but, if I'm the only person this is working on, I suppose it would be better if I at least know what's going on. It is going to take months for me to get used to the fact that, not only do I have a family, but they are super freaking rich too. It's not crazy either but Dad still has shares in many fortune-500 companies that bring in a lot of money and he made a lot off contracts when he was still officially alive. Leyna also works online as a maths and physics corrector for exams and makes her own money that way. She even has a couple of patents that bring in a slow flow of cash.

For the rest of the day, we were looking up all the interesting stuff we could get with a top spending limit so high I would rather never get near it. It's crazy what we can find online, especially that we are not just using the normal online shopping places. Leyna surfs parts of the web someone her age should run away from; actually anyone should run from, there are dark things out there. It's actually quite exhilarating and makes us totally overlook the time until I hear Dad calling us up to the lab over an interphone I had not even seen. We head up the stairs and find him waiting for us like a happy child with a new gift.

 — 'I figured it out, what they were putting in your bodies and more specifically why it would never have worked.' He starts before dragging us across to a bank of monitors on which I see a load of numbers I don't understand.

— 'What do you mean dad, these numbers don't add up, it would mean that he has over a hundred different DNAs that's impossible!' Says Leyna before I get to even understand the first lines.

— 'Due to the way they had set up their lab, they had to use very powerful hormonal suppressants on all these otherwise horny teens. Thus, the catalysts that they used to fuse the DNA were left dormant. Now that your bodies are finally off the suppressants, you should actually start to see things happening. I mean, in the Petri dish it certainly is doing more than I have ever seen.

— So, are you trying to say that I'm actually going to change physically? And what about Byeol-I?' It bothers me to think that she went through the same trauma but that the results will be null for her.

— 'It's not sure what the true results will be but I'm quite sure that, within the next weeks, we'll start to see changes if they are going to happen at all. It has never been done using this technique before.' He smiles at me and then adds. 'Don't worry Son, no matter what we'll be here to help you and make sure it all goes well.' We discuss all the possible outcomes and, in the end, he adds something momentous. 'If you want, Stary, I could use my son's blood to catalyse yours but the risk of that is that you may not really want this, I mean it can be pretty horrible in the end, we don't even know what is going to happen.' Says dad half-heartedly. It scares me to think that it could go terribly wrong but, at the same time, I suspect it would at least have been well worth all the pain.

Before we head down for dinner, Dad gives me the choice of giving my blood to catalyse Stary's but she refuses and says that she would rather not go through with her hybridisation. He also admits that he is not sure it would even work but at least had to offer. That being out of the way he gives me two synthesised hormones, testosterone and interestingly enough some oestrogen as well. As strange as it sounds, he told me that for some reason my body is actually producing both male and female hormones in equal amount. I really don't know what all of this means but one thing is for sure, I am guessing that I may end up being both male and female. As far as I know, I only have male genitals but they are also not exactly developed as they should be. Cross-Gen somehow made our minds and bodies not even know what we are.

Three days later dad takes us out in a really cool looking minivan, it's fully electric and has an autopilot system which he immediately puts on and it is set to take us to Glasgow. When I ask why, Leyna explains that they have all their mail sent to a variety of PO boxes in the country and, for this much stuff, it had to be the biggest one and thus in the largest nearby city. Because the van is self-driving, we spend the entire trip chatting and discussing what to do next. Stary asks something I would not have expected, she asks if she can go home to her parents. Dad immediately says that he is fine with that but that I can't go with immediately.

— 'You both have travel documents and if needed I can get you both new passports made. I would prefer it if you stay home Falawk, we have no idea what will happen with you.

— If I were to go with, it would not be for a while and thus I do think that Byeol-I will need to travel alone. I could join her there in some time but not for now. I only just found my family; I want to stay with you guys for a bit.' That sounds rather egocentric but it's hard for me to even think that I have a family, I have no desire to leave them now.

— Don't worry Falawk, I would actually prefer to go alone, facing my parents is going to be hard enough as it is, I don't really want them to start having strange thoughts because I get there with a boy.' She looks a little down when saying that but I totally get it, I mean I find it hard enough to deal with my having a family, I can't imagine what it must be like for her who knows she has parents but that they shipped her off to Cross-Gen and basically left her for dead.

— 'According to their website, Air Korea has a flight leaving Edinburgh tomorrow night, I could get you a spot on that one if you like.' Says dad after looking the flights up on the minivan's tablet.

— 'Waou, that would be great! If it's okay for you, I would really appreciate it.' She replies very happily.

— 'Sure, I'll book it for you on the way back, we are here.' Says dad as the van goes back to manual and dad parks it.

We get out and have a short walk to the post office and, although they are discreet about it, I see that both Leyna and Dad are on their guard. I don't want to ask why but, then again, it seems logical as they are both supposed to be dead. We get to the post office in no time at all and with nothing suspicious happening. The packages are not many but two of them are rather large and I find it rather fun that half of the smaller ones are just from Amaze-one and fBay. Leyna ordered a bunch of components so that she can help me out with my choice of stuff to learn, in this case electronics and programming. I want to do that so that I'm not just becoming another geneticist in the family. Nena, the kind lady from the post office seems to know a lot more about our little group than I would have expected. She hands Dad and Leyna a bunch of letters that are stamped with an obvious 'deceased' sign. Interesting, I wonder how she knows to give them letters that were withheld as their recipients are supposed to be dead. Dad introduces me to her and she is somehow very glad to meet me. Once we have all our mail, she tells Leyna and Dad that the route back to the van is clear and then walks out with us to help carry all the mail and boxes. As we cross the road to the van, an SUV comes barrelling down the road and straight through a red light, it stops just a few metres away from us and three guys jump out. Before I even have time to react, I hear the crackle of electricity and feel a burning pain in my side…

Close Shave

When I come back to my senses, I'm in a strange-looking room with a lot of loud voices outside. This immediately makes my Cross-Gen induced survival instincts kick in and, before I even know I'm doing it, I'm huddled in a corner, probably looking scared out of my skin. I hear the voices calm down and then my dad walks into the room, sees me in the corner and runs over and hugs me.

— 'Sorry son, I've been arguing with the police for the past twenty minutes to let us just go home. They want me to declare the Cross-Gen attack as a political attack on the country but I think they could just pass it as gang violence.' He talks so fast that I nearly miss some of it, my head is spinning from all the adrenaline I must have produced.

— 'So, wait, they want you to claim that Cross-Gen attacked the country by attacking us?' That makes no sense, it's not like we represent the country in any way.

— 'Well, if I reappear as alive, I can claim your mother's murder against them and thus state that they attacked a scientific emissary for Scotland which equates to attacking the country. But this is not at all what I wanted to do and definitely not what I planned as my return to the world of the officially living.' He almost seems disappointed that things aren't going his way.

— 'It's not the worst that can happen, right? And where are Leyna and Star? Are they okay?' I realised they were not storming into the room so I wonder what happened.

— 'They took the van home so that Star could get ready to fly, with this amount of danger potentially around, I want her as far from us as possible for her own safety. Thankfully, Nena has a car and accepted to take us home. I'm still trying to figure out why they were targeting you only, they didn't attempt to tase any of us which actually played in our favour. Leyna knocked two of them down and I go the third.' Okay wait what, my adorable little sister knocked out two huge goons from Cross-Gen. Well, I'll make sure not to piss her off!

We discuss logistics and, in the end, the head of the police department comes in with a bunch of files and asks my dad to testify anonymously about the attack. Later, he also says that Dad only has a week to get his things in order and then he has to state his 'aliveness' to the world. You would really not expect that to be a subject of conversation that would come up with your dad but hey, these past few days have been full of surprises. Another surprise is added to the list when I see my dad picking up the phone in the room, dialling a number and asking Nena to pick us up. I ask him why he doesn't have a cell phone and he just smiles saying that it's hard for dead men to pay for bills. That just bothers me, how is the house running then I wonder. I mean it's not like there is a lack of electricity or water. I'm about to ask about that when he just says that we can talk more once we are safe out of here. Nena gets us and drives us to the outskirts of the city before we stop at a mall and dad tells me that from here, we drive one of his cars that he stashed away. I'm a little suspicious of this until I remember the autopilot function that the van had and figure this car probably got here like that too. We thank Nena for her help and dad gives her a hug before we drive off in opposite directions.

With night upon us, the autopilot system starts running on ultrasound and radar to get us around at full speed. Thus, we are driving lights off in the night at speeds far above the legal values but it feels great and gives us time to chat a bit.

— 'You said you can't pay bills but then how on earth are you still able to power the house? Let alone have water go to it?' I ask still wondering about that.

— 'That's easy, as those bills have always been paid, there has never been a need to prove I'm still alive. It's only difficult if I want to open up a new contract as they do background checks. Also, most of our electricity comes from solar on the roof and the water is all pumped out of the wells.

— Waou, that's actually really cool, I didn't think that you could get such a big place off the grid but I guess between you and Leyna there are enough PhDs in the house to go around.

— You forget that both of us are specialised in genetics, your electronics studies are actually the first ones that will be useful to the house. All the house's current infrastructure was setup seventeen years ago not long before I died. And yes, I love saying that, it made me sad for years but now I love it.' Yeah, Dad, I already figured you were super strange don't worry.

— 'Has it only been you and Leyna for all these years or does she at least have friends she hangs out with and stuff? She is still super young even if she is far too smart.

— Yeah, we hang out with Nena sometimes, she was really helpful with the girl stuff for Leyna, she actually used to work in town by us but her transfer to the post office in Glasgow was very useful even if it meant she no longer came over for dinner as often. She will come Friday by the way.

— It's not like I had friends at the orphanage other than Jenny and Laura but Laura was adopted and I have no idea what happened to Jenny, she was still in Cross-Gen when I got out but they were rapidly culling at that point so she may be out somewhere. Do you think you could find her? I didn't even think of that but it would be great if we could find her again, I mean for all I know they could have killed her. I seriously hope not.

— I can try and see if there are ways of finding her via the satellite networks and the dark web, maybe Leyna can help track her down. If they released her, she has to have appeared somewhere, right? Can you remember enough of her to give me photo details. However, we are nearly home and we need to help Byeol-I get ready so that we can head out to the airport tomorrow at sparrow fart.'

We drive in through the gates and, as they close, I see them glow for a second and before I ask Dad just says that they are electrified at all times. I can't believe how much of a security system he has set up here but it's really impressive. Upon arriving at the house, the carparks itself and we go into the house. I find Star fully packed and just about ready to go take a bath with Leyna and myself. She seems half happy and half scared to go but as we head to the bathroom things get awkward, I've been having a slight headache for the whole day but, just as the steamy bathroom opens, the heat is enough to knock me over. I just fall over dizzy and pass out.

When I come to again, it's dark and uncomfortable, I'm lying on something really hard and quite cold. As soon as I try to move, a stabbing headache hits me flat and I feel dizzy again. A loud beep noise makes me want to turn my head but I can't. I'm starting to wonder if it was all a dream and I'm just back in Cross-Gen, it feels like it, my arms are tied down and so are my legs and chest.

— 'Don't move too much son, you have a concussion. You're healing stupidly fast but you still need to stay immobile for a few more hours.' Comes my dad's voice as he walks into the room.

— 'How long have I been out of it? Did Star leave yet?' I ask. She was supposed to fly super early and it was nearly midnight by the time we got home last night.

— 'Yeah sorry, you were under for nearly twelve hours, she should be taking off by now.' He replies.

— 'Damned! Why did I have to miss that and why did I pass out?' I ask that rhetorically but get an answer.

— 'Your memory block is gone so your mind is being overwhelmed by flashbacks. Chances are, if you think back to your childhood, you'll be able to remember it all by now. And by the way, when we can, I would like to scan your blood again, something is changing on your skin.' The way he drops both of those pieces of information is rather scary.

I try my best to ignore the pain as I immediately try to look at my body and see that my hairs are darkening at a pace I can almost see. It's a strange change but it certainly is one and I'm absurdly happy to see that something is happening. As much as I don't want to admit it, the idea that spending two years under constant torture and maltreatment was not fun, but thinking that it was useless was devastating.

He was not lying; the memories are all there and they actually feel like they always were. It's just then that I realise why Leyna had a hard time not jumping at me when I came in, I knew her. She was already turning 6 when I was taken out of the house. Dad had explained it all to me too, he had done it because otherwise I would not have anything nearing a normal life, the people in the village would ask far too many questions, I was not supposed to be alive. The car attack that I always thought was an accident comes back to me and I realise I was in the car, I didn't get hit too badly, though, just a few bruises, I was at the back of the car and in a very secure booster seat. I can't have been older than three at the time thought which makes me wonder when Leyna was born. With these memories flooding back into me now, there is but one thing to do, grab my little sister and give her a huge hug. I'm sure she is going to want me to tell her all about our mother as she never knew her.

As for my body changing, it looks like the only change for now is my body hair. It's growing out faster than I would have thought possible and is dark, probably black but it could be a dark brown. I'm thinking that, if this is just the beginning, there can be many more changes. Maybe I'll really become a hybrid in the end, who knows. It looks like it's going to take a lot of time too. There are no antecedents to this and, although my parents made the transversal genetic system, they have no idea if it ever worked so it's not possible to guess how far the changes are going to go. I just want to know if I'll even still look human after all this works out or not.

— 'Falawk, you want to come see this.' Yells my sister up the stairs calling me to the tech room.

— 'What's up? Did something bad happen?' I don't really know what to expect but the images on the screen are certainly not what I thought I would see.

— 'Cross-Gen caught up with Byeol-I it seems, she was stopped before take-off and taken to an interrogation cell. Said cell got blown up two minutes later killing five police officers and Byeol-I who was found to be under protective custody. I'm sorry bro, I don't really know what to say. They are trying to figure out who did it but nothing obvious has been found although they have stated it was definitely her that was targeted.' She looks at me and just gives me a hug not knowing what more to say. I don't know what to do either, I didn't know Stary that much. Although we survived Cross-Gen and running away together, in retrospect, I actually didn't know much about her.

— 'Leyna, Falawk, we need to lockdown the house. Sorry I saw the news, there is no ways that they are not going to check here. Martin, the head of Cross-Gen knows I live here, although he thinks I'm dead. I've alerted the authorities through a series of tips but we need to put up the security. That means we can't get out of the house for the next five days, at all.' He sounds rather flustered and that takes me off topic.

— 'What sort of defences do you have here? Do we have guns or something?' I ask, kind of fearing the answer.

— 'Automatic turrets by the gates and down the drive as well as spaced out through the forest around the house, the fence around the house is high strength steel and it's now electrified. It's also topped with razor wire. I have security cameras everywhere in town and here, we also have a radar jammer and anti-missile system and if all else fails yes, I do own a certain number of manual weapons.' Well, now that is a real freaking arsenal.

Dad takes us to another room that has a sign 'control room' on the door and, in there, we see the setup he has ready. Two walls are covered in monitors cut up into sections, each dedicated to a camera someplace either in town or here at the house. Some are even heat sensing and most seem to be tracking motion too. On another wall are bows and quivers of arrows, somehow, I'm guessing those will come in handy soon enough if they make it to the house. I really hope they don't even come this far, if possible, can they just forget about us entirely please. No such luck, I see the vans crossing the one street in town that I've seen and somehow just know that those belong to Cross-Gen. How they got this many vans here

I don't know but, clearly, they mean to rat us out and, following them on the cleverly set up system, I soon see them closing in on the house.

'Systems are on and running, we just need to see if they are going to bother contacting before they try and break in. It's all on camera and it's also being live-streamed to the police. As much as we don't have authorisation to kill them, there is nothing saying we can't bludgeon them with thousands of rubber rounds. Only the bows and my rifle are lethal, oh and the electric fence too but that's beside the point.' Says dad pointing at a screen that shows a map of the property with status information on the fences and ammunition levels of the turrets.

The day ends with no hiccups and, so far as we can tell, there is no activity whatsoever. We all three head to sleep with the alarms set on high so that, should there be any movement, we would be alerted. It goes on like this for the five days that dad wanted us to wait and, as soon as it's past that time we reduce the house's security and turn it into a night only thing. It's rather hard to not think about there being a risk, as we know, there is one but we can't exactly live in constant fear, we need to go shopping and so on. I've not even had time to really process the loss of my co-escapee yet. Somehow, the constant fear is preventing me from processing the whole thing.

We decide to go all the way to Inverness for shopping and it's just Leyna and I going as Dad needs to stay home to protect the house. It's a good thing the van is self-driving because I don't think I would be able to drive it properly otherwise. We take it, take enough cash to get groceries for about two weeks and we also order a load more things from online platforms and get them shipped to the PO boxes.

Changing

For days, weeks and soon months, we build up a routine of going to different cities to get shopping done. Dad somehow manages to get me to do my licence so that I can legally be driving the car or van and he even manages to figure out a way to track my body changes without being invasive. I have a diary and write down all the changes using the day of my return home as day zero.

Day 17: My body hair seems to be growing out a lot faster than I would expect, we are wondering if this has something to do with my sudden surge of teenage hormones.

Day 29: I woke up in utter pain today, I can't really explain it but it feels like my bones are shifting and changing shape, it's been going on for a few days but it just got worse and very painful.

Day 30: The pain got worse and I have a bulge at the end of my spine and it hurts to touch it. Dad is saying it's a bone formation.

Day 31: It's getting so bad and I feel so weak that Dad has me on an intravenous nutrition pouch with a low quantity of pain killers. As this is all new science, he is worried that anything stronger will affect me negatively.

Day 33: I passed out yesterday, no idea at what time but I certainly know that it was from pain. The changes seem to be happening faster and at the moment I don't really have a single part of my body that is not tingling.

Day 47: I couldn't really write much for the last two weeks; my body has been in far too much pain. There is a lot to say, though, I seem to be growing a tail, my bones are getting lighter apparently and my muscles are shifting around a little. My teeth seem to be growing into fangs and my eyes are also changing. My irises now are no longer round but rather a sort of cross shape halfway between cat and bird eyes. The most notable alteration to date is in regards to my ears, they are changing shape and somehow moving. I have no idea how any of this is possible and neither does dad. Although hybridisation works like this between animals, it's never worked with humans, until me.

Day 73: Well, it's been a while, my body is still changing a lot and I've been partially bedridden since the beginning but it's somehow getting better now. My ears, back and growing tail are currently the most painful things on my body. My eyes have totally changed and my vision is far beyond normal now, I can see in the dark and somehow zoom in if I will it. I've had lots of time to practise this and it's useful. All my senses are getting much more powerful, to the extent where I can hear the low hum of electricity in the night when I open my windows and listen towards the fence.

Day 113: Yeah, it's been a while, I had some sort of sensory overload and dad had to put me into an induced coma so that I wouldn't scratch my skin off or go crazy. Now that I woke up again, I have a lot to say. So, first things first, my hair has grown out a surprising amount, it's down to my waist and most of my body has now got a decent amount of fur on it. It's all white somehow and that really surprises me, I have always had dark hair and now all of a sudden, it's white. Beyond that, my eyes have changed into their new form, they really look like a cross and they are even more sensitive than at my last diary update. It's crazy how many details I can now see. My ears have moved to the top of my head and grown into points and now look very much like fox ears. My limbs have slightly changed but mainly my muscles seem to have shifted around a little and, I'm pretty sure, if I train, they will be rather insanely strong. Oh and, uh, I don't know how to say this … well firstly I have a very nice bushy tail now and it's really soft and to be honest I don't know how I lived without it for so long. The thing I'm really not managing to say is about the parts of my body that I never really cared about until now that they are different. It would seem as though I am becoming or have become hermaphrodite. I should probably say intersex but I feel a little too animalistic at this instant to use such a human word. I seem to now have both genitals and that is really very strange. Because of the orphanage and later Cross-Gen, I never really felt like a man but still, now that I somehow became intersex, it's even more bizarre. Dad apparently had to help with a few of the changes on my body, my nails become a little more like retractable claws for one thing, my new genitals another.

Day 117: Today is the first day in nearly three months that I was able to actually walk around properly and even go outside. It's damned cold out there yet, somehow, I don't feel it anywhere near as much as would be logical. I even played in the snow with Leyna and Dad. Thanks to that, I discovered just how useful my tail is. Dad has been telling me that I may retain both physical genders as my genetics seem to be both but I will only ever be able to reproduce as a male. Somehow that is very comforting I really didn't want to think about that but at least it's cleared up. According to Dad and Leyna, my genetics are very interesting and somehow Dad thinks that I may be the only true hybrid as my genome really mutated in every part of my body and even my immune system is totally overpowered but accepts its new form without attacking itself, according to them, that's a rarity.

Day 123: It's been just under a week and there has been one new thing I saw. My weight had gone down a lot but it's now rising quite rapidly as I hit the gym daily for hours on end and running in the snow helps a lot. Because of the amount of fur I have, clothing is becoming a problem so I tend to be naked. It's not like anything is visible, my fur is far too thick. My sister keeps on asking dad to catalyse her so that she can become a hybrid too and he will soon. He thinks that, because she is my sister, he can use my blood as a base for a catalyser that will actually work.

Day 137: Today Leyna had her first catalysing and, just as horrid as Cross-Gen, that meant hundreds of needles going into her skin, muscles and bones. It was horrible to hear her scream in pain and somehow, I could actually feel it, like some sort of phantom pain. Somehow, though, after we did all of the injections, Dad said that this will be the last time we need to and that, thanks to some biochemical engineering, he made is so that the hybridisation process is much slower and that way, if all goes to plan, it will take a year or two rather than just a few months.

Day 150: It's the last of the six months that dad said I would need to be quarantined and today and tomorrow will be spent adapting clothing for my new hybrid form as well as making hats to hide my ears. It's somewhat crazy to think that I'm actually the first of my kind, there are no others like me on earth and there may only ever be a few. Also, much to our collective surprise, there has been no sign of activity from Cross-Gen for the past months. It would seem that, after the attack on the airport, they are trying to lay low before something big, it's like the calm before the storm.

Well, now that I realised just how incomplete my notes are, let me give you an actual description of what I look like now starting at the top and going down. I have pointy ears on the top of my head like a fox or cat would, they are, like the rest of me, covered in fur. My hair is now at my waist and is Snow White, I like having it plated by Leyna so that it is manageable. My eyes are green and gold with cross-shaped irises. My face is not fur covered other than my now growing beard but it's trimmed to look normal. My facial shape is a lot more angular and even a little elongated giving me a very fine but feline look, kind of like an elf, I guess. My back has thicker fur on it and my chest and belly much finer and softer. Thanks to my hours on end of sport and my rather remarkable endurance, as well as a very special diet we developed in-house, I have put on a lot of muscle but it's not bulk rather power. As mentioned earlier, I have a very bushy tail that has taken me some time to learn to use and control properly. To be honest, I'm still learning, I was not born with the right instincts. The bits between my legs that I'm sure you're wondering about, well with a little bit of very fine surgery performed by my dad - yes, I can't believe I let him do that to me – I now have both male and female and they are surprisingly both functional. The surgery was just to help my body adapt as it could obviously not purely create something out of nothing although it kind of did. As for the rest of me, well my legs are insanely strong and thus I am fast, faster than humans by quite a bit. I've been practising jumping between trees to get used to my tail for balance, my newfound strength and my surprisingly light body weight. I'm one metre eighty, sixty-five kilograms, my bone density being lower yet stronger than it was, not sure how that works. Oh, I seem to have a rather large amount of reptile DNA too as I heal extremely fast.

Now, with all of that said, we made me a few sets of clothes I can wear to go out, comfortable pants that hide my tail, a long sleeve top that is loose enough to not make me too hot all the while hiding my thick fur, a hoody and head band combo that hold my ears down and hide the fact that they are even there. It is a pain to wear headphones or even earphones so Leyna is busy designing some new ones for me. With all of that done, it's finally time for me to go do my driver's test and then we can actually go out with Leyna and go shopping and stuff without constantly risking being pulled over. That is set up for next week so I've been practising out at night with Dad and Leyna. She can already drive but, because of her age, she can't get a licence, dad just taught her to make sure she would be able to get away in case of emergency. My over-powerful strength and hyper-sensitive senses mean that I am both a very careful driver and also a bit of speed junky so I have to keep calm all the time so that we don't get fined.

It only takes a few days for me to have everything I need memorised and soon I'm on my way to get my licence. It's almost just a formality at this point considering how much faster my body reactions are there is nearly nothing to worry about.

And I was right, they gave me my licence after asking to take a photo, well that was a bit complicated seeing that I had to take off the hoody and then the headband I first had to prove to them that my fox ears were real and then I had to deal with them losing their minds over that for a little while. Somehow, probably a call from one of their higher-ups that Dad knows, they accepted it and just took a picture and made my card for me. The only hassle with this being that, now, there is a record of my new hybrid form and that means that Cross-Gen will be able to know I am alive and that I'm the first ever hybrid.

Accidental Reveal

It's been about a month since last time I wrote anything down as nothing really happened, I mean sure I had to deal with a load more physical things but nothing major, more like realising that I could actually have my period… Yeah, that's a thing and let me tell you guys, you should really respect girls, it's no fun when it just starts hurting like you've been kicked in the nuts. That took a few days to get used to and, thankfully, Leyna was an amazing sister as always and looked after her older sister/brother. It's kind of funny because I feel like I'm more of a woman now but at the same time I know that I'll never be able to carry a child but I can make one with a woman so I guess I'm still a guy. This is going to take a lot longer than expected to actually get used to that is for sure.

Today I decided I should start writing again as it's my first long trip out with Leyna and we are driving all the way to Newcastle upon Tyne in England. We are going for a long one-day drive; we chose this option simply so that there would be less risk of Cross-Gen being nearby. It's going to be a really fun road trip, I think. I'm actually looking forward to driving a bunch, it's always fun to exercise new muscles and driving is something novel to me.

We head out at 9:00 and soon realise that a four-hour drive to get food is quite a long one. It's a darned good thing we have autopilot and a large refrigerated box in the back to put all our groceries. The drive is going to be long but it will be worth it considering the fact that we can talk and sing and have fun for the duration of it. We are getting to know each other much better these days, especially because of all the time she spent looking after me during my transformation time. She is far ahead in her schooling, getting another PhD soon. She is amazingly smart and, thanks to her coaching, I was motivated to study as much as I could and try to catch up to her. Our discussions are thus quite lofty as we are discussing everything from quantum physics to popular psychology. Don't think that we don't also talk about other things but, as I was never really a proper teenager and she has always been raised at home, friends and parties are not really a possible choice of discussion. We did decide that I should go to see Byeol-I's parents and tell them the truth behind their daughter's death so that will be happening sometime soon. It has been nearly ten months since she was killed and, although I barely knew her, it still hurts to think about it. We talk about that quite a bit; Leyna says she wants to travel with me so we start planning that and we also have to plan the negotiations with Dad. It's not like we have a private jet so we are going to need to fly normal commercial airlines and that may be difficult considering I need to stay hidden.

Halfway through our discussion about that, Leyna decides to call Dad and simply ask him if we can go to Korea for a few weeks. He hesitates for a few seconds then says he will look for flights and make sure Leyna has a passport as soon as possible. From there, he does go on to say that we are going to need a cover story and immediately lines us up for three conferences there that he wants us to attend while we play tourist for the rest of the time. The call goes on long enough that we get to the shops right after hanging up, put the van on charge at one of the charging spots and head inside.

This shopping centre isn't exactly huge but it's still quite a decent size and should have a few things we don't need but that we are surely going to take home anyway. Leyna reckons we need to get some more clothing for me so that we can modify it for the trip. She also wants to get more ingredients than usual because I've been eating us out of the house since I've been able to deal with real food again. My new body needs a lot of food and specifically a lot of meat and other protein. I think that, because of my mixed genetics, meat is going to become the centre of my diet.

Shopping goes rather fast and, thankfully for my cover, no one seems to look twice at my clothing although I'm walking next to my sister who is remarkably beautiful and wearing a nice and colourful short dress. I ask her if I can get some girl clothes and she agrees that, because of my changed body it would be rather logical. We spend quite a while looking for some which turns into the most fun part of the trip as it takes a while to realise that, should my tail be let loose, my clothing size is much smaller than it was. It would seem that, although I have regained a lot of my weight, I have actually got slimmer and thus am now far smaller in many ways. We remarked that I don't have any breast growth making some clothing really not possible as they require a balcony I don't have. The next few stops are all for food and, once that is done, we finally head out of the mall for the last time. We have emptied two trolleys into the van, one with clothes and other needed things; now we are headed back to the van with enough food and non-perishables to last a long while. As we walk out of the mall, cross the road to the second parking lot where the van is, I smell smoke and immediately my sense go into overdrive. There is a building on fire and someone is screaming that there are still people blocked inside. The building is creaking and starting to fall and I can't hear sirens so the firemen are still far. I look at Leyna and she just nods telling me that I should act if I want to and, of course, I do. I take off my long pants and undo my tail from the straps holding it down. Drop my top off as well and there, in the artificial light of street lamps, my white fur glows. It takes only a few strong strides to have the building in sight and then, from one side of the road to the other, I jump straight into the first-floor window. The fire licks my fur and immediately singes some of it but it's somehow not that painful. I follow the screams and find four people grouped in a corner of a room, they see me coming and first freak out before I tell them to calm down, put one on my back and one in my arms and jump through the window. It's a good thing my legs are insanely strong, I catch our joint weight, put them down and jump back up to get the other two. Although I was fast, by the time I have the other two out they are already passed out from the smoke. I can hear the ambulances in the distance, that should mean they will get treated in time. I ask the two that are still awake if there is anything or anyone else in the building and they only ask me if I can get their safe. A few jumps, a lot of surface burns and singed fur, and some rather vicious tugging and I have a safe out of the building. As soon as the ambulances arrive, I make myself scarce but not after having made sure that the two who passed out are actually alright and then I need to dash before this attracts Cross-Gen or media. Everyone saw my fur, my tail, my ears and, of course, my eyes. Leyna gets me into the van, with adrenaline now running low, the pain from the burns is starting to hit and it's pretty bad.

We head straight home and before we even hit the main roads dad is calling, apparently my 'little stunt' as he calls it is on TV and radio and internet. Now the entire world knows that there is a hybrid running around in the world. By the time we are home, the world media has got hold of the story and many people are asking to interview the 'saviour fox man' as they are calling me. Dad seems almost too calm about this and simply said that, although it's a little faster than he wanted, it's time to tell the world that he is alive. That implies we are soon going to be seeing a load of people which doesn't make me feel particularly comfortable. There are so many things I'm not okay with yet, one of them being the fact that I feel very uncomfortable about my identity. There is no actual stable thing in me yet, not even my physical or mental gender is fixed yet. We will be going across to Glasgow to talk to the BBC tomorrow morning. No one other than the person talking to us is aware of our coming, for security purposes they don't want me to reveal myself until we are safely in the live room. They are going to be the first and hopefully only news outlet to get hold of us and from them I'm sure it will spread like wildfire. The next couple of hours go by in a blur; between getting all the clothes packed away, getting my burns treated and bandaged – which is hard because of my fur. The good news is that most of the burns are already healing - dad says that has something to do with my reptile DNA - somehow, I got the ability to heal really fast. Leyna helps me choose an outfit and we end up going with a pair of nicely modified pants and a button-down shirt. I was tempted to wear a skirt but she talks me out of it as we may totally freak people out if we do that. A nice long bath and chat later and the two of us head to bed. It's not the first time I have this feeling yet, at the moment, it would be nice if there were at least other hybrids out there that could join this madness. Leyna's only change for now is in her eyes, seems like that is the first thing to mutate. After one short night of sleep, I get up, Leyna helps me change my needed bandages and remove the ones that have already healed. She helps me by braiding my long hair and then we get dressed and ready to go. We are meeting the journalist at 10:30 and it's almost time to go if we want to be there on time. According to the information given, we'll be on BBC Global live TV so that's going to be interesting. After a quick breakfast, we are in the car and off to Glasgow. For some reason, Dad drives quite a bit over the speed limit – although he is hiding it rather well – I think he is quite stressed out. We are doing at least 150 km/h in a 110 zone and he is showing no sign of slowing down. I just hope we don't get pulled over or caught by a fixed radar as both would cost a lot. Once we have pulled into the underground parking of the BBC building, a single person, a lady, comes to us and ushers us to an elevator.

— 'It's a pleasure to meet you Mr Rogue, Master Rogue and Miss Rogue, thank you for agreeing to this interview.' She says in a very polite and strong Scottish accent.

— 'Thank you for having us and please, use our first names, no need for all the formality.' Replies dad with a shy smile.

— 'Considering you have your tail and ears visible, Falawk, I suppose you don't mind appearing like that on live TV? I don't plan on having you guys touched up, you did a good enough job yourselves.' She asks me. I nod then add.

— 'No reason for me to hide something everyone already knows about at this point. It's also very uncomfortable to hold them down and out the way.

— I can hardly imagine but I do believe you. We have arrived, we will be live in 10 minutes so that should give you time to read the questions I will be asking before we go in. No one is aware of your coming they only know I managed to get an interview with an important person and family.'

We get ready, make sure our clothes are not crinkled and then read through the questions, they are quite open-ended and allow us to take many tangents and add details. They really planned this out so that we could reveal only as much as we are comfortable with – that's nice of them, I guess. When we are called into the live room I hear the first gasps, the camera people, the small VIP audience and even the other journalists. Everyone starts taking pictures and the flashes seem to blind me once and then, all of a sudden, my eyes somehow adjust to the bursts of light and seems to cancel them out. We are invited to be seated on one side of the large table that serves as the presentation desk. As soon as we are ready, the teleprompter says: 'introduce yourselves'. The journalist we met earlier introduces herself as Eleonore, she is the lead reporter for this branch of the BBC. To her right is a well-respected local geneticist from the Edinburgh University, he greats dad reverently, guess they know each other. Then dad introduces himself simply as Dr Iring Rogue, Leyna just as Leyna and I go with Falawk Iring Rogue. Of course, my official name is Falawk but I do have to add the fact that I used to be called Haiylen. With that out the way the questions start:

> — 'So, Dr Rogue, you and your wife were the first creators of the human hybridisation theories, yes?
> — That is correct though we never did manage to reach physical mutation, only mental and immune ones, that is before my wife was killed.
> — You say killed; do you mean the accident we all read about was in fact orchestrated?

— Yes, it was, by Martin Herjeune the current head of Cross-Gen. Until this moment he thought I was dead too, I faked mine and my kids' deaths that day. Well, Leyna was actually born right there and then as our car was burning up.' I didn't expect Dad to give that many details but, when I see the gasps and horrified faces of the journalist and VIPs, I understand why he did it. 'Seeing as how my son was affected by the loss of his mother, I then set up him with a fake name and had him put in an orphanage in southern France. I thought this was for the best but, in retrospect, I think it was maybe not that good. However, from there on it's his story to tell.' They all look at me expectantly so I go ahead and tell them about the orphanage, my friend who went with me to Cross-Gen and whom I still have no information about. I tell them all the dirty and horrid details not caring that they will need to beep out some swearing.

— So, Falawk, you are the first and maybe only successful hybrid, do you know how that is?

— No idea, sadly I think that it was just a fluke, I had dad run hundreds of tests and nothing is panning out. I'm just, different, somehow.

— Are you worried there will be others who will go through the pain and suffering you did?

— Of course, there were hundreds of us in that first room, some of them are bound to become hybrids I suppose. They are probably out there right now, or in the Cross-Gen centre. I really hope that, after people see this, they will stop sending their kids there and that, hopefully, the world governments will act against Cross-Gen in a timely fashion.'

We go on discussing the possible changes on others, I'm asked if some can fly and simply reply that I don't know. After another few minutes we are invited out of the live room and a few photos are taken before we get back to the car and then rapidly out of here.

My First Trip

Since the media thing, it's been about three weeks and things are still crazy but somehow Dad figured that this is a good time for me to travel. I've been wanting to go to Korea to see Byeol-I's parents and tell them what happened even if, by now, they probably know. My main reason to go there is to present my condolences and, whilst I do that, I need to find out how they managed to get her to France to be part of the program. We need to find out just how far Cross-Gen's influence and power stretches. The most important thing we need before we try and shut them down is to know what we are really up against. Leyna still really wants to come with me but Dad has vetoed that rather vividly. Although he originally was onboard with the idea, that was before I made us be revealed to the world. He has been keeping her life a secret for long enough and – even now that we revealed ourselves to the world – he has no desire to put her in harm's way. Planning a trip, when you need to make a new passport, all new photos because of many physical changes and when you have to find out if there will be restrictions from the destination country, is a complicated process. I've been writing to the embassy in London representing South Korea and thankfully they were really nice and, although I don't need it, gave me a tourist visa that will make my status easier and allows me to stay there a bit longer if I want to.

A few weeks of preparation later, looking for a flight and setting up a few other things on the way; I think things are finally ready for me to go. One thing my little sister told me to try, was to offer students to be interpreters for me and surprisingly one of them actually accepted the offer. Her name is Hayannah and she even agreed to help me learn some basic Korean whilst I am there. That being ready to go, I downloaded a bunch of audiobook courses and a few pdf courses for the 15-hour flight and got ready to go, packing the strict minimum and the one thing of Byeol-I that I still had, a lock of her hair. It's rather strange to think that I'll be delivering that to her parents – a couple who sent their daughter off to a crazy program just to 'make her better' – I mean really…

The day of the flight comes and I'm off to Edinburgh international airport a good 4 hours early to make it there nice and early. Against my will, Dad got me a first-class seat, apparently it was really not that much more expensive but I always feel bad just using money when I don't need to – I guess that's left over from the orphanage. Needless to say, this means that I get to board in priority and I also get to order whatever I want for food ahead of time and thus asked for a steak. Once through customs, which took ages because they first didn't believe that I was really who I said I was and that my ears and tail were real. I made it rather obvious when I accidentally growled at the one worker and displayed a beautiful set of sharp canines, they somehow figured it all out rather fast after that. Waiting for the plane in an airport lounge is boring so I decided to shop around in duty-free for some traditional stuff to give to my translator. Leyna booked 2 weeks of her time and I can't just pay her cash, it's much nicer to give gifts too. I have enough spending money to live comfortably for a few months should I decide I want to stay there a bit longer so we'll see how things turn out. My first port of call is getting the whole condolences out of the way; there is no need for that to weigh me down for the entire trip. There are so many things to see and do there and I may be able to pick up a bit of a new language if I work on it so there is that too. Upon being called to the gate, I board early and make myself nice and comfortable in the plane just waiting for take-off. I brought hours of Korean lessons with on my phone – Dad and Leyna set me up with a nice new smartphone which I've been playing with a lot – so I'll be listening to my courses and doing as much as possible of the work that goes with it. Thankfully, I'm used to cram studies, that's what we did back at the orphanage as we had no other choice. You know, even when I should be focussing on the late Byeol and meeting her parents, I still can't stop thinking about my friend Jenny. I hope Dad will be able to figure something out to get the kids out of that lab. Starting my lessons just as the doors seal shut and we get ready to taxi and take-off, they start nice and easy so I speed them up a bit and work my way through the first two hours in one shot. By the time I'm done writing down what I want to, my meaty meal is brought and I manage to say thanks in Korean to the air hostesses, eliciting their congratulations on my pronunciation. Obviously, the news about my existence had made it around the world because she responds 'You're very welcome Mr Rogue' in Korean. This language really sounds nice so I'm certainly looking forward to being there.

The rest of the many hours of flight I spend between sleep and learning, mixing both up into a nice little routine until they announce the second meal and approaching landing. Fifteen hours of flight and a lovely 9-hour time difference makes me really want to sleep more but I think there will be much more to do upon arrival than just that. To avoid attracting too much attention, I tie down my ears and hide my tail as best as I can – just for the time between going through customs and going out into the arrivals area. Upon walking out, a blue-haired girl about my age is waiting for me with a little bored with just Haiylen written on it, Leyna had decided that would be the easiest way to be discreet about who I was for a few minutes. I walk towards her and greet her in Korean.

— 'Anyeonghaseo, you must be my contact. Falawk Iring Rogue, at your service,' I say with a small bow.

— 'Good evening Mr Rogue, I am Hayannah, I'll be your guide for the two weeks. Shall I show you to your hotel?' She says in a beautifully cute English with a slight twang of Korean accent. I had no idea she would be this cute, well I guess this is going to be a nice two weeks.

— 'That would be lovely, do you know the way by car, I was planning on renting one or would you recommend I do that later?

— Later is better sir, the traffic is rather bad, we will use the underground it's much faster and safer.

— Understood and please, call me Falawk or anything else you prefer you don't need to sir me, I'm barely your age.' She smiles at that and calls me 'Yeou' saying that it means fox.

After we get onto the underground, she asks why I hardly have any baggage, I only have a small suitcase and my backpack. The only reason is that I felt like getting local clothing and also because I really want to travel light. Most of my nice clothes are modified to allow me to hide my appearance but that seems to not really be needed. I do tell her that, as soon as I get out of the metro, I really want to let my ears and tail loose.

— 'Would you mind if I see them? I still can't really believe that you are a hybrid, I mean you're even wearing contacts to cover the awesome eyes you had on TV.' She is kind of hyper about her question but I don't mind.

— 'Sure, of course, I was going to treat you to dinner tonight anyway so I need to shower and change, can't go all stinky vixen around town now can I.' Oups, I just gendered myself female, hope she doesn't pick that up. It's been happening more and more recently but I am not yet sure if I can actually get away with it.

— 'Vixen? You're a girl? I thought you were a guy?' She looks really puzzled, her beautiful dark eyes staring at me.

— 'Long story short, I'm both but I feel a touch more female at the moment, it depends on my period and yes I have one of those … never thought girls suffered that much until I became one.' I smile at that last part, thankfully my period is only in a week and a half, that helps a lot.

— 'Waou, that has to be difficult to live with, although I barely know you, if you need anything girly just let me know okay, it can be awkward for you to buy it yourself.' Dang she is considerate. Little sis really found someone amazing. We looked together but, in the end, Leyna is the one who chose and I'm glad she did.

We get off the metro, head up an elevator and are almost immediately flushed into the crowds of people but still manage to make it to the hotel I'm booked into. I specifically asked dad nothing fancy so he found me the only two-star in the area near where Hayannah lives. The hotel staff give me my room card access and I clone it into my phone and give the key to Hayannah, she may need it for some reason, you never know. We head up together – I ask her if she wants to head home or just wait for me – she chooses to wait so that we can go out as soon as possible after I'm ready. As soon as I reach the room, I am peeling off my clothes and getting ready to shower. Releasing my tail is certainly the first thing I wanted to do, getting rid of my clothes a close second. The slight gasp in the room reminds me that I'm not alone but I just turn to her and ask:

— 'Do you want to shower too?' She shakes her head looking away and that's when I start wondering …
— 'Sorry, am I doing something socially unacceptable? I really have little to no understanding or knowledge about social norms, not just here but anywhere, I lived my life in an orphanage and then a lab, sorry. Please feel free to tell me off if I do something wrong.' I feel extremely sheepish and, although my fur is hiding the little part of me that shows I was male, I still wrap a towel around my waist.
— 'It's not exactly normal to be naked with someone you just met, that's about it. I understand you are now a girl and all but you still can't just do that. So please shower

alone.' She seems slightly flustered so I excuse myself and head to the shower.

Still having not learnt to take my time, I run through the shower at the speed of sound and am shaking my fur dry within minutes. Getting out into the room, I take care to cover up the potentially bothering parts and rummage through my bag, grab some adapted clothes and put them on. Adapted means they allow my ears and tail free and don't require underwear. As soon as I'm dressed, I use some of the Korean I learnt and say I'm sorry to Hayannah. Through her surprise at my usage of her mother tongue, she forgives me. We then head out to a restaurant she selected as being a good source of meat. It's not like that's all I eat but, after my hybridisation, the amount of protein my body requires is much more. Through the streets of Seoul, we walk and, let me tell you, a hybrid is treated the same everywhere: like a strange creature no one understands. A lot of the passers-by actually said 'cool cosplay mate' thus proving that they think my tail is not real. It doesn't take us very long to realise that we have a lot of things to talk about other than my hybrid nature which is a relief. She is quite interested in learning more about my educational background and that's when I have to admit to not really having one.

There is little that could have been greater than the sheer amount of food and chatting that went down today. I have no idea where I found the energy, yet I managed to recount most of the past couple of years – in some number of details – while preparing for a detailed explanation of the hybridisation process and what it entails. Hayannah is really interested in that and actually admitted that she would somewhat like to be a hybrid herself seeing at how many advantages it comes with. At some point, we headed from the restaurant to a coffee shop and then from there back to the hotel. Hayannah decided that, in return for my kindness in treating her to meal, she wanted to introduce me to a local alcohol called 'soju'. It turns out that was all we needed to get into an even deeper conversational mood exchanging about everything. From tales of mean people in school and university to her telling me about her very extensive list of friends – while trying to convince me she is introverted. It was quite an enlightening time and actually lead us to the early hours of the morning.

Through the wrist band Leyna made me and my phone, I updated HQ quite a few times and told them that I'll be fine. They have a permanent monitor on my vitals as it is so there is that. It should help to keep them reassured. It also means I can know if there are any new and relevant changes to my health or if there are any more changes to my body. Now, after taking my new friend home, it's time to crash for the night.

Unpleasant Conversations

After a great night of rest, I finally had the time to quickly get myself ready for a trip to one of the more remote parts of the capital as well as a very unpleasant conversation. It's never nice to talk about death but it's even worse when you have to tell people their child is dead; or at least I would think it is. In my mind this is going to go one of two ways, either they will be very sad and mourn, or they won't care as they had originally got rid of their daughter anyway.

Meeting up with Hayannah in the late morning, we head to the car rental place and deal with the paperwork together. It would seem that the black credit card I got from Dad has a lot of motivational power when I need to do things like rent a car. This is how we went in with a card and out with a car. Hayannah was rather surprised I have a licence and I had to admit that it was not exactly obtained the normal way but I do know how to drive both a manual and an automatic car. From the rental agency, we went towards the address Leyna found for Byeol-I's parents. It's soon time for me to have my, admittedly undesired, chat with them. I still have no idea how this is going to go. The GPS reckons it's going to take about an hour to get to the destination so we slip back into our conversation from yesterday.

— 'So Falawk, you said that you don't really understand social norms yesterday but didn't you live in that orphanage for a long time? Did you not learn them there?' Asks Hayannah with an inquisitive smile. She seems to have busted my crappy excuse for what happened.

— 'I don't really know how to say this. That was the best excuse I could come up with at that time. What I should have said is just that I needed to get my clothing off as fast as possible because it was clinging to my fur and was very itchy. I'll admit that I also got used to always being with people, male or female, when cleaning myself so I thought to ask if you wanted to join. I didn't actually think it through, sorry.' It's hard to admit that, after the lab and being back with my sister has got me used to someone with me all the time and I kind of miss it when it's not there.

— 'Oh, well, I guess that makes sense. Next time just say it, I would have understood but also left you a little more privacy if I had known. It's not too much of a big deal but, a little warning next time please.' If I have to guess, I would say she is blushing and that makes me really wonder if I was revealing myself way too much there.

— 'Sorry again about that, I'll be sure to warn you and get changed in the bathroom next time. Also, before I forget, you said you were interested in the idea of being a hybrid yesterday? Were you serious about that?

— Oh, very much. I would love to be one considering the awesome perks it seems to come with. That being said, I understand that it also has a lot of problems with it too because people are really not mentally prepared for this sort of thing yet, are they?

— Nope, not at all. They tend to react very strangely when they see what I look like and I don't know if that will get better even if there are more of my kind. And yeah, I don't know if I still qualify as fully human so there is also that part that makes this situation a lot more difficult to deal with.

— Yeah, well that is the one thing that makes me unsure about it but then again there will be less xenophobia once there are more hybrids I would think.'

So, our conversation goes on and on for the entire drive. We discuss everything from the presence of hybrids in the world to the risk I am taking by being the one to announce Byeol's death to her parents. By the time that actually becomes a real concern, though, we are there and it's time to have a possibly very unpleasant chat. I walk up to the door of the small town house and knock on the door softly at first and then a little harder. I still have no idea how strong I am so this is a rather difficult activity because I need to not break the door down.

When Byeol's parents open the door, they are first inquisitive as to who I am and what I am delivering but then immediately understand when they see my ears and tail. This lets them know – not only that hybrids are real – where they sent their daughter actually did something. Thus leading to me doing what I came here for and telling them what happened with Hayannah helping with translation. When I tell them their daughter died, their only reaction is to say, 'Well she was a failure anyway, dead is maybe better.' This leads me to promptly swear at them in Korean, Aetherian, English and French. Before I can cause any physical harm to them, Hayannah puts her hand on my arm and simply pulls me away softly. Her gesture is such a calm and soothing one that, even in the height of my anger, I can only listen to it and follow her away from these horrid people. It's a good thing, in some ways, that there were no remains left for them to burry because they probably would have simply thrown them out.

— 'Well, that was far more terrible than what I expected. I honestly can't believe there are people like that in the world. I mean, their kid died. What the hell.' Hayannah is actually about as angry as I am.

— 'They did decide to send their kid to Cross-Gen after they found out what kind of treatment the people there gave out so they clearly didn't care about her. You're right, people like that should not be allowed to have kids.' We get into the car and I don't even turn on the GPS.

— 'Do you want to go somewhere? I mean, I need to calm down, anywhere I can go and explode a little?

— We'll either need to go to the Sea or to a mountain. Drive east as far as you want and then stop when there are few houses left. I'll just warn my parents I'm not coming home tonight.' She texts her parents quickly and then we just start going east.

That drive's conversation was rather stale, neither she nor I knew what to say but we soon found a place to stop and take a break and let off some steam. With Hayannah's permission, I took off my top and the long pants I was wearing favouring a skirt I had in my bag. This lets my tail roam free and also means I feel a lot more comfortable. The pent-up anger I had turned into me punching a log straight into a rock face and shattering it on impact. I guess that means my strength is now really a lot more than it was before. Interesting, but also terrifying for the poor girl with me who didn't expect the huge explosion of anger to come in that form. Without even thinking about it, I just take off at a full sprint and jump onto a branch high in the trees and then run on the tops of the trees at full speed. I'm so glad it's nearly dark because this would really have called for a mediatic scene, I'm sure of that.

Holidays

After that outbreak Leyna found us a place to stay – after frantically calling me when my heart rate spiked – she thought I was in danger. We decided to make it at least be nice so we drove a little further east to the sea. My sister made us a hotel booking there with view on the crashing waves. There were a lot of different options for the booking but – as I specifically asked for Leyna not to spend too much – she got us a double room, as in two single beds in a single room.

After a decent dinner, and a short walk on the beach, we head back to the room and Hayannah goes to shower first. She didn't bring a change with her so, while she soaks in the shower, I quickly run out and get her some underwear at the convenience shop, thank goodness these exist. They didn't have much that looked nice but I got her the best there was. I also got some other basic supplies and more soju. I lay the clothes out for her right by the bathroom door and quickly turn around for her to be able to privately get them. Next, when it's my turn to shower, she actually remembers the previous time she was there, as in yesterday, and tells me to soak and take my time. This is an order I can accept and I take at least 5 minutes in the shower this time, longer than usual for sure. My fur is glistening from the shampoo, it is really nice whatever it is. It makes my fur feel so soft I actually want to not wear clothes so as not to spoil it. That being said, I was asked very kindly to not be naked in front of my new friend, so on goes the cotton.

— 'Do you mind if I come out with just panties on? I really don't feel like wearing more than that with my fur this soft, it would be a waste.' I ask through the closed door with a sheepish voice.

—   'Sure, I am only wearing a tee-shirt and pantie too, as you said, you're basically a girl too. Come on out Yeou, I've got the soju and snacks ready for us.' That's reassuring, I guess she doesn't mind too much after all. So, with the towel hung up and only a rather skimpy black pantie on I leave the bathroom and rejoin Hayannah in the room. She has turned the lights off and left only one small light on and is sitting on the one bed, a small table between the two with drinks and snacks ready.

—   'I guess this means you don't mind staying up all night?' I ask gesturing the table content while I sit on the opposite bed.

—   'A bit of sleep would be useful but sure, we can enjoy. I think you need it quite badly.' She opens a bottle of soju in a rather fancy way creating a little whirlpool in the centre of it. 'Hold your glass, I'll pour for you.

—   Thanks.'

We go on to drink our way through the four bottles I brought, finish all the jerky and other snacks in due time too. At some point in the conversation, Hayannah asked if I needed a hug and that led to what is currently the longest cuddle I have had since that birthday at the orphanage.

The next day, at the break of dawn, when I wake up, I find Hayannah hugging me, fast asleep. Without waking her I get off the bed and stretch, she kind of slept on top of me in a way. I hope this doesn't lead to anything awkward, I would hate to spoil our budding friendship because of a bit of anger that turned into a drunken hug. Before she wakes, I get dressed and head out of the room to buy breakfast and go for a quick run on the beach. There are but a few elderly people on the beach at this hour who don't seem to worry about my presence too much – until I start running along the waterline, barely breaking a sweat as I dash at over 30 kilometres per hour – then they point a little more. The nice thing about my hybrid form is that my entire body is rather light – my strides hardly impress into the sand. It must look like I'm flying over the sand.

After a quick stop through a cafe to pick up some pastries, coffee and hot chocolate, I go back to the room and drop it all off. Hayannah is still sleeping and that gives me time to shower off the sweat from my run and make sure I am ready for whatever happens today. The shower only takes a few minutes, then it's time to wake sleeping pretty girl and serve her some food.

— 'Hayannah, it's time to wake up. I've brought you food.' I say to her from the edge of the bed. 'Hmmm, hug.' She says without even opening her eyes so I oblige without thinking, hug her and softly lift her into a sitting position. 'You're soft, you're like a teddy.' She goes on saying.
— 'Thanks, I guess, do you want some breakfast?

— Yes. What is there?' She is starting to wake up a little more at this point it would seem, this means that she is also aware of the fact that she is still snuggling her face into my neck. She pulls back really fast and says 'sorry' in a small voice.

— 'Don't worry about a morning hug, you slept hugging me so it's fine. Actually, I owe you my thanks, I would have not slept so well if not for you.' She looks at me with big eyes as I give her some breakfast on the table between the beds.

— 'I'm really sorry, I overstepped a lot last night. I should not be taking a job like this one and then ending up sleeping in your bed. That is wrong on far too many levels. I'd better tell Leyna so that she knows not to pay. I'm so sorry, I'll leave you alone.' She is really going on a guilt trip by the sounds of it.

— 'Hayannah, you did nothing wrong and you helped me a lot already. Thank you for keeping me company after the events of yesterday and please don't just leave. That would really not help and I don't want to ruin the beginnings of our friendship because this was a so-called job.

— But it's so unprofessional. I can't believe myself; this is so unlike me in every way.

— Hayannah, please, breath, don't worry. You did nothing wrong.

— It all feels wrong, how can I make myself forgiven for this? I mean what can I do to make it right?

— Towards yourself or me?

— You Falawk.

— How about we start our friendship again and this time take a chill pill? I made a blunder on day one and you on day two. I'm still here for at least two weeks and I can make that more.'

After what feels like at least an hour of negotiations, she finally calms down, eats her breakfast. She then decides that the best way to make up for this situation is to give me a non-exhaustive tour of Seoul. So, here's to me hoping this is going to lead to as many shenanigans as possible.

It's now been 10 days since and we have been to most of the major parts of Seoul and even a few areas nearby. Things have finally settled between us. This means that Hayannah is now okay with being around me without looking down. We're also at goodbye hugs in the evenings when I've taken her home – I even accidentally met her parents too. They were rather surprised about the fact that I'm half-and-half gender-wise. That confused them almost more than my ears, tail, fur and all that. It would seem that intersex people as still really underrepresented in society.

We've been discussing whether I should stay in Korea longer or not. Admittedly, I have nothing else to do for now so I could, at the same time, I kind of want to go to university so that I can get a few degrees, especially in genetics for obvious reasons. In light of the requirements I need to meet before I can register in university, I have little choice but to go back to Scotland for the time being. Of course, I don't really want to leave from the comfort of my nice holiday in Korea to go back to university immediately – so the best I can do for now is enjoy my time here, follow Hayannah to class a few times maybe too – during this time I can figure out where I want to study.

Travels

After about three more weeks of searching for the correct place to study, sending a million and a half emails and making far too many phone calls, we managed to get me set up to go and study at the college of biology and the university college of electrical and computer engineering at Edinburgh University. It's now only a question of getting back up to speed with the research in those fields. I also need to freshen up general studying skills as well. There are a lot of things that I have not kept up in the lab and even after, things most students need and successful students really must master. Even if I have had the opportunity for the past few weeks to observe Hayannah and her classmates, this doesn't mean I'm ready to go and study science all of a sudden.

A few days later, Hayannah and I are on our way to the airport again, our nice time together coming to an end. Things have finally got really comfortable between us, mostly, I think, due to the fact that she doesn't see me as a typical male and thus not a threat. This has led to late night chats that ended with nice hugs and even the occasional cuddle but nothing much interesting – this can and probably is due to my absolute lack of knowledge of human interactions. If Cross-Gen did one thing right, it's to have killed my social knowledge. I am mostly relying on the people I see around me to know how I need to act and what I should do. This time, on the subway, I have a little more with me in regards to baggage as I am taking home a decent number of snacks and gifts for my sister and father. I also am not hiding my tail or ears any more. I have already ended up on a lot of media here so there is no real reason for me to hide any more. One other, much more important, nice thing, at this early time in the morning, I have a head on my shoulder as Hayannah sleeps softly. She is dead tired, we stayed up until nearly 2 a.m. and had to get up at 5 to get on the subway. Her dad had kindly offered to take me but I thought this would work out better for everyone and it's the same sort of travel time anyway. Getting to the airport, a trolly comes in handy to help with the bags and then we are off to the check-in. With my bags checked and my passport ready to go, I have a full hour to kill before my flight.

Hayannah and I thus head to the lounge area and get some light breakfast to share and a ridiculously strong tea blend.

— 'You know, you can come visit me anytime you want. There is definitely enough space and I would love to introduce you to my little sister in person.

— That would be awesome, I just need to save up quite a bit for that kind of trip to be possible.

— I'm pretty sure we could figure something out but you are right, these long flights are pricey.

— Speaking of which, don't worry about the second part of the payment, you treated me to food almost every day for the past weeks. It's more me that owes you.

— Not sure my sister, who manages the finances by the way, will agree but I'll ask her. And your company was more than worth it. I came here hoping it would be nice and you made it awesome.

— No need to flatter, you are pretty cool company too. That being said, I didn't think I would get so comfortable with you. To think I would cuddle and hug you. Doing those things was a nice memory for me.

— Likewise. In fact, I hope I can steal a last hug before I go.

— You could steal more than that.

— You mean a kiss?' I say that without even thinking but, at the same time, it does feel like the next step. I really like this young lady and there is no reason to hide that.

— 'I meant more than one hug. But.' She is looking down and her heart is beating so fast I can hear it from across the table. What did I do to this poor Hayannah. Hopefully nothing bad. 'I would not mind a kiss too actually.'

Our conversation comes to a halt before I lean over the table and give her a very quick and soft kiss on her lips. We both smile and then simply finish our breakfast talking about everything and nothing. The hour we have quickly comes to a halt when an overhead announcement calls for me to go for a suitcase inspection. Hayannah immediately offers to come with so that she can help me through whatever procedure this is going to be. There is a very clear sign to the section of customs where I need to go and, once there, the person at the desk calls in for me to go to my bag.

A very stern-looking officer comes to usher Hayannah and myself down a corridor going off behind the front desk. A few turns later and I'm not sure how many doors, we finally stop in front of a much sturdier looking door and then the officer tells us to go in.

'Falawk Iring Rogue, Haiylen Glas, Subject YC503-FWTL-D, you belong to Cross-Gen and should never have tried to leave!' Exclaims a loud voice right before I get hit behind the head.

Inside

What now?

Pain. That is the first thing I register. Cold. The second feeling. Hunger. The third.

Opening my eyes is a struggle. The light from the room I am in brings its own fair share of pain too and immediately makes me shut my eyes. Although my new eyes can adapt to light, this is beyond their capability it would seem. There is something wrong, something very wrong with me.

Where I am?

I force my eyes open again and that's when I see that I am lying naked on a bed that looks far too similar to the ones at Cross-Gen for it to be a coincidence. Without moving, I focus on each part of my body assessing the damage my captors have already done. Yes, I guess that, after that rather obnoxious announcement right before I was caught, I am now a captive of Cross-Gen. Again. Well, that all being said, it would also seem like they had a lot of fun with my body too. I can clearly detect a broken toe, bruises all over and, it would seem like they also had other kinds of fun consider the pain I feel.

For some reason, though, my mind is staying horribly lucid. I would have expected myself to be in shock or something but I just feel numb. Maybe they are experimenting their drugs on me, that was after all what they loved doing.

'Ah, you are awake. Good. I have a little gift for you.' Comes a voice overhead, through some sort of intercom. After that, a video starts playing, projected on the wall. It's the moment when I was captured, viewed from inside the room. Just as I got knocked out immediately and moved to a side of the room to be striped and beaten, they held Hayannah to watch it all happen. That already makes my blood churn but clearly it was not going to stop there. Oh no. They then grab her and violently sit her down on a chair before tying her to it. 'My favourite part is coming. You really should not miss this bit.' Says the voice again. And just then, someone pours a bottle of something over Hayannah and then everyone except the person filming, leave the room carrying me out. She is screaming as hard as she can for help but no one seems to hear her. 'No one is in this part of the airport; it is under construction and it's the weekend. Now, why don't you scream a little more for him.' Says the person filming, whom I realise is the person talking overhead. Just as he says that he throws an open lighter at Hayannah who immediately catches fire.

Those screams of fear and pain will never leave my mind, I know that for a fact. Especially not after the sick person showing this to me replays that scene five whole times before stopping it. I am too choked up to move but again, for some reason, it is not affecting me anywhere nearly as much as I think it should. 'Don't worry about you feeling numb, we want you like that. You've caused us enough trouble as it is, there is now no reason for you to enjoy emotions or anything else for that matter.' Says the voice.

I'm then left in absolute silence, in this horridly bright room, to deal with all of this. But not for that long; truth be told, I have no sense of time here so it could have been a long time. Food – or something that I suppose is food – is slid through a trapdoor in the door with a command coming overhead, 'eat'. Well, I guess this is certainly Cross-Gen, it's the same robotic voice that we all hated so much at the centre in France. I can't help myself; my body is forcing me to eat as it is clearly hungry. The stuff tastes like nothing in particular which makes me wonder what it actually is but that thought is rapidly replaced with satiation. Somehow this horrid porridge is making me feel very full.

Well, great, they are drugging me. I just woke up strapped to a board, arms and legs spread, in Adam's clothes.

There are loads of things around the room but the most noticeable of it all is the table full of medical tools next to me. Lovely, this is some sort of torture chamber.

— 'I see you are awake. Good. Let us begin.' Comes a voice next to me. I find I can't turn my head as it has been strapped in as well.

— 'What do you want with me? Why did you have to hurt her?' I find myself screaming out. Interestingly, my mind is still numb and surprised by my outburst.

— 'Oh her. That girl saw too much but don't worry, my men got rid of her a fun way. Now, as for you, I hope the drugs are enough to make you tell me: where is the key?' What the hell does he mean they got rid of her? They killed her…

— 'The key to what?

— Hybridation idiot. The key to make it work!

After that things turn for the worse. The man talking to me is rather unhappy when I tell him I have no idea what he is talking about. This leads to pain. He starts by threatening and then actually starts hurting me. First, just by hitting me but it soon gets to sharp objects. I must have passed out because, when I open my eyes, I'm back in the bright room with baby crying noises playing on repeat.

…

These torture sessions repeat a few times but soon the man gets crafty. Using bubbling hot wax, he starts ripping off strips of my fur. Of course, nothing he does will make me know the answer to his questions as I never knew there even was a key.

...

Today is different, they have me naked and furless and take me outside onto a helipad. That's when I see what is next, cold. It also tells me we are somewhere in mountains. They collar and chain me to the railing and then leave me there. Just as I thought I was going to freeze to death, some person comes out and throws boiling water on me. Their drugs must really be messing with my mind for me to only acknowledge these events and not even react to them consciously. It's almost like my body is driving itself and I am a mere bystander.

...

Today is different again. After they left me alone long enough for the burns to scab, peel and heal, someone takes me to a different part of the building. This time it's back to good old Cross-Gen methods as they stick me with needles, remove a few muscles fibres and even draw bone marrow.

...

Looks like I passed out again. It must have been for a long time because my fur is growing back. It's surprisingly no longer the same. It is now a dark auburn almost brown colour and seems to be differently making tufts as well. There are also small scales appearing in some parts of my body, especially around my eyes and around my elbows and my knees. It's almost like my body is mutating to defend itself against the pain. Interestingly as well, there seems to be less pain now and my thoughts are clearer allowing me to think properly. I wonder if they took me off the drugs they had me on. There is going to be no getting used to this entire system as they keep on changing it. On top of that, and contrary to the centre in France, there are no other prisoners here so I can't even talk to anyone.

At this point, regardless of how horrible I look – covered in scars badly hidden by my fur – I can't help but wonder why they haven't come back for more? It's as though they completely forgot about me. Now, this gives me some time to assess my state and all the damage that has been done. Interestingly enough, my hybrid nature comes with very good regenerative abilities as well as a great number of other healing particularities. Most of the really bad incisions that were made are already fully healed but have a very fine sheen of scales on them. This is preventing my fur from growing back on those areas thus making the scares even more visible. My face was left mostly untouched except for one large scar that I can feel across my nose, probably related to them

146

breaking my nose at some point. With the drugs they pumped into me, the torture happened a lot while I was unconscious thus making me think that they had me in a state where I could respond to questions but not remember what they did. They haven't done anything more to my reproductive parts, something I sadly expected to happen a lot. That being said, after the massive number of blockers from the France centre, I suppose they just hate sex. I don't really know what they did to me in those regards but I don't feel particularly good about it either way.

With my now auburn fur, scars and bushy tail, my appearance can only be considered animal at this point. I don't see how I could still pass off as human. Faint steps are becoming louder now so that means that it's time for the next part.

After they decided that my rather lovely auburn fur was not allowed, waxed it all off again and left me naked in the pain room, something finally happened.

'It was your blood this whole time. The key was simply your blood. Now we just need to suck you dry and put you out in the cold to freeze. You're finally going to die, you wished for it so many times and here it comes.' Starts a voice before it is acted upon. I am tied to a table and needles stuck into my arms and legs taking out what must be at least two full litters of blood. I guess this is how I die. Thank you for reading my memories like this dear reader, it was lovely knowing you all this time.

The cold

It burns.

It's cold.

What?

How am I still thinking?

Am I really still alive?

But why is everything so cold?

They must have put me out in the snow on the helipad or something similar because I can see the outline of the building behind me. I was left with no clothes, no fur and no blood. This is not going to end well but, considering I am still alive, it's probably the one and only time I can try to run away.

Getting up this time feels like the hardest task to ever be accomplished. The lack of blood in my body is keeping me from functioning even slightly. I also have to be careful that I am not spotted too fast. They may have left me out to die, I'm pretty sure that the leader person doesn't want me running – of should I say limping – away. It takes me a few tries to get upright and a lot of tries before I can start moving but, once I do, probably from the desperation of looming death, I manage to limp forward at a decent pace. It's nowhere near the speed I was at right when I was becoming a hybrid, but at least it's something. From there on out, only a few things cross my mind: how fast can the cold kill me? What will happen if they spot me? Will I get anywhere?

Never in my life did I think I would become the living definition of frostbite but here I am, freezing to death and, just to make it worse, I think I can hear snowmobiles behind me. I can't possibly have gone far, not in my current state. Their sound is getting quickly nearer and louder. Incessantly, they get nearer and soon I hear the first shot. They are not even bothering with silencers at this point. I hear the loud bangs and the whistle of the bullets as they miss me. My instincts take over and, despite my physical state, I start running. This time it's actual running, not quite at my full hybrid speed but that's pretty normal considering the muscle atrophy from the torture and lack of protein in my diet for the past I don't know how long.

Regardless of how fast I think I'm running, there are no ways to outrun a bullet. Even with their aim being so far off, I soon receive my first hit. It goes right through the top side of my right ear. Any bit lower and I would not be narrating this any more. The adrenaline in my blood, because, yes, it can only be that, seems to be stopping the pain from really registering. I keep running until another bullet enters my shoulder. Now that one I feel.

I'm not sure what happened and how I got here; my body is sliding down a snowy and rather steep cliff. They must have hit me again but I can't tell where, the cold is making me far too numb. The slide comes to an abrupt end on a rocky outcropping that catches the popsicle-creature-thing that I am. So, this is how I die, with bullets in me somewhere, naked, bleeding and yet frozen, in a place no one will ever find me.

A temple

Uh.

Excuse me?

I'm not dead?

But, how?

Those are the first thoughts that cross my mind when I open my eyes and realise that I am not dead. Well, saying that this could be the afterlife too. It's a stuffy and hot place, it smells amazing and yet horrible and there is some sort of aftertaste in my mouth that I can only describe a green tea.

Moving my body seems pretty impossible and yet, it somehow works. The moment I do start moving, though, I immediately realise that there is something very wrong with me, something has changed. My entire body is covered with the auburn fur. It was never this tint and it most certainly did not cover my body this much. It's as though dying made my hybrid genes even stronger; they are now only really showing their full power. My tail is back too, oh, I guess it's not, it's better than before. It's now a very luscious auburn tipped with a dark onyx black. The tip is so dark it almost glows. I wonder what colour my hair is; auburn as well but with streaks of white and black. This is becoming a very interesting situation. For both my hair and tail to have become this lighter auburn colour and my skin to be covered in similarly coloured fur; this can mean only one thing: the trauma caused my mutations to become even more pronounced and now my body has finally been able to deal with all the changed genetics. This must mean that I am now truly showing all my mutations to their fullest. Reaching up to the bullet wound in my right ear, I can feel the contours of a pretty decent hole there, it's a little jagged but at the same time, that's all it has going for it. My ears are at least bushy and fur-covered again which makes me a lot more comfortable. I can't tell where the other bullets hit me or if I still have damaged body parts so I guess it's time to get up and figure out where I am.

It's so much easier to say that than to actually do it. Considering that there is no way of knowing how long I was out for, I should really expect it to be a lot more difficult than just getting up. I almost immediately crash to the floor and that's when I hear the footsteps. They are not those of a soldier or a westerner even, these are shuffled steps, fast and delicate on the wooden and stone floors. The door creaks open and immediately a call for help is shouted out. I can't imagine how strange I must look, naked, covered in fur, and stinky, to anyone who is not used to seeing a hybrid. There have got to be about 10000 reasons why this person screamed but I did not expect it to simply be for someone to come and help him lift my sorry self up. They are speaking in a language not many have heard before and at that, probably a very location-specific dialect. The two monks, for yes, that is what they are, lift and carry over this furry creature that is I to a room with steaming hot water flowing into a large stone bath in the floor. Slowly lowered into the water, they then proceed to wash my fur and hair in the most delicate and kind way it has been done since my sister.

Sister. Whatever drugs they had me on must have been fully flushed out of my system because I can finally feel emotions and thought normally again. My sister must be worried sick at this point, or she thinks I am really dead this time. They did quite a number of making it look like I was dead, for sure. One of the first things they did was remove the bracelet that was tracking my vitals, it was gone when I came to in that room. Without really thinking of it any more, I realise that communication with my benefactors and saviours is going to be needed. Trying to speak to the two monks, now with lightly damp deep red robes, in English doesn't help. Not only is my mouth too dry to articulate sounds they simply nod at me and make an 'x' with their hands. This could mean that they do not understand just like it could mean they are not allowed to talk to me.

With the bathing done, they help me into some very soft fabric underwear – no reason for them to know I hate underwear – and then they garb me in a very floaty red robe like theirs. To my surprise, they have already made a hole for my bushy tail to fit through so, with a surprisingly nimble movement, it pops through and happily wags free of restraint. I'm only now realising that they are both men and I'm somewhat both sexes; I do hope this has not been a problem during the time they were looking after me. It's also possible that the Cross-Gen people fiddled with that in ways I don't really want to know about. Thankfully, it would seem that enough trauma makes one forget things or at least the drugs they had me on did something to that effect. It would be rather nice if I could at least thank these two monks for their help so I give them the best bow I can manage in my current state and then, unexpectedly, nice-mister-monk-on-the-right pats my head softly and says something that I can only interpret as 'it's a pleasure'.

A monk on either side of me, helping my weak steps along, we go through a series of corridors and arrive at a large dining room full of other monks. There are not that many, maybe about thirty red-robed ones and a few in white robes and one wearing golden threaded red and deep auburn. The monk in the golden robe seems to be the one with the most authority here as, when he stands, so do all the others. A simple sign of his hand and I am brought in front of him. One of the white-garbed monks comes besides me as I am sat down in front of Mister-in-gold. The kind red-robe monks disappear to the tables and everyone is seated again.

— 'I will translate for you and his excellency. Please use common English or Chinese, I do not speak other tongues.' Says Mister-in-white. Thank goodness someone speaks English here.
— 'That is very kind of you, thank you. Thank you to his excellency for harbouring me and for having taken care of me.' I respond through a croaking voice. Immediately, without it even being spoken, I am served some steaming hot tea and motioned to drink by the head of the house. The tea seems to be healing me instantly almost as it runs down my throat and soothes the pain therein. As the cup is put down, so the master speaks.

— 'His excellency asks for you to introduce yourself and to explain what you are, where you are from and why you were so hurt in our sacred grounds.' Translates Mister-in-white.

— 'My name is Falawk Iring Rogue, first human hybrid in the world. I am the product of very advanced science and I was hurt in your sacred grounds because I was running away from captors who were torturing me to find out how to create more hybrids.' Keeping these answers simple is quite a challenge admittedly but it also seems to be the best idea. Translations are made and responses come in.

— 'Do you know the answer those people were looking for? How to make more like you? Also, are you a man or a woman?' Ah, so it is a bit of a problem, good to know.

— 'They found out, while they were hurting me and experimenting, that my blood contains a special trait that allows hybrids to be created. As for my sex, I am both. This was one of the effects of becoming a hybrid.' Once that is translated, the head monk looks at me and somehow looks very sad.

— 'His excellency says that, if his diagnosis is correct, you were very badly harmed and it will take some time still for you to recover. He is offering to keep you here and, in exchange, you can help us all. You will have to respect our rituals and ways and you will need to help as much as your recovering body allows you to.' There is no way not to accept such an amazing offer. Although it is very cliché,

I wonder if these monks have their own martial art I could learn too.

In this manner, our conversation goes on for a little while longer before I am helped back to the table of the red-robes and given a wooden bowl filled with soup. It is mainly mushrooms and some vegetables but is also somehow thick and filling. It's quite easy to see that oil and meat are things that are not very common here. In many regards, this is a great improvement for me considering oil was recently used to try and cook my skin; that's not really an experience I wish to repeat any time soon. The food is rapidly feeling me up but also seems to never end. It's as though someone is constantly filling up my bowl when I look up or away. Maybe I should stop looking at the rest of the room, especially considering they are not really taking much notice of me regardless of the strange creature I am.

With the meal done, I am approached again by the kind translator and asked if I feel alright enough to come and observe their evening rituals. Both in thanks to their kindness and out of plain intrigue, there is no way I am saying no to that. He leads the way, out the dining room, into a room full of thick and warm coats – one of which I am handed – and then out into the biting cold. The first ritual is already taking place and it comes in the form of a series of martial arts movements and paces which all the monks, even the oldest ones, are executing with ease. They say the names of each movement – or at least I believe that's what it is – while doing them and so I learn both the names and the forms. Trying to copy said forms is, however, a much more challenging prospect and one I struggle with quite badly. Thankfully, these kind hearted people don't seem to take this as an opportunity for laughter and rather simply show me again and again until I can do them right.

After these are done, everyone goes back inside except for a few who tend to the huge fire pit that must be the source of heat for the entire building. I wonder where they get the wood from this high up in the mountains; I doubt they have a thriving forest anywhere within walking distance. As even the last monks usher into the warm interior, I get a glimpse of the night sky and stars. This is the first time I could lay my eyes on them for what feels like forever. Seeing as I had far too much time in the orphanage, I learnt a few star maps and the only constellation I could always remember was the Vulpes one, constellation of the fox. Not only is it visible in this sky, all its friends are there too and it seems as though there is no stopping the number of stars here. What is immediately more important to me is that I can't really tell where on Earth I am based on these stars; maybe learning those maps a lot more in detail would have been a good idea rather than just using the knowledge to show off to Jenny and the others.

Once back inside, through some keen translation and a bit more guiding around the building, I am taken to a dorm room where I will be staying with all the other Red-Robe monks. Because of my hair length and fur, they have decided to not request that I shave off everything like my roommates must. This is the only lenience I will get during my stay here; all other rituals, practices and work I will have to complete. They never allow anyone into their monastery without a lot of prior training and vetting down the mountain in one of their sister temples but, due to my condition, an exception is being made. For now, however, it's bed time.

Rituals, Work, and Recovery

It has now been about three weeks since I woke up in the recovery room. Thanks to both the kindness and expertise of the monks here, I have recovered to the point where I can at least fully function. There are still a lot of aches and pains and, on top of everything else, wounds that are taking a long time to heal. Regardless, I am happily going about helping in the gardens and in the various other red-robe rolls I am placed in. Recently, as in two days ago, I was deemed fit enough to help with the wood gathering. I've really wondered how this works and found out in a pretty awesome way.

Right nearby the monastery there is a very deep valley and cave system leading off from it. This is where a lot of their sustenance comes from as it is deep and clear enough for a large number of things to grow. The way to get down is, truthfully, terrifying. They built a series of pulleys and zip-lines that go all the way down as well as rope ladders and stairs. It's pretty much a case of choose how fast, in what manner and where you wish to die. The first two monks go and then it's my turn. They both took the zip wire and it does seem somewhat safe so I go with that option. One very exhilarating – actually slightly slower than expected – ride later, we are all ready to start working. The trees here are plenty and the rule is to take only what we need and always plant back as much as possible. The little valley still has quite a bit of space and so does the huge cave mouth so we transplant a lot of the tree sprouts before gathering some of the dried wood piled in the cave and cutting two more branches into logs to replenish the stock. Then it's on to mushroom gathering and that is quick and easy: Take all you find but always leave two per spot where you get them from. The harvesting part is in many ways quite fun and the monks show and teach me a lot too. Their language and dialect are becoming easier for me to understand but it seems that I often miss out on the nuances of what they are saying. With the most important part of their ways being directly linked to a god I have never heard of and their arts all dedicated to said God; it is a little complicated to really understand the meaning behind their words as it is often in references to holy texts.

When we get the harvest done and all is loaded into sets of baskets, it's time for the hardest part of this adventure:

getting the goods and us back out of the valley. The quick way is to take the rope ladder, the safe way is to not be here in the first place, or at least take the stairs and the really fast way is to do what is the craziest thing I have ever seen. Without any prompting or warning, one of the monks took two baskets on his shoulders with a pole and then jumped onto one of the zip wires and started running up it. Not only is his balance extremely good, he is doing this at rather intense speed too. The other monks look at me and we all just choose the stairs. Mister-Wire-Runner obviously gets to the top fast and gets back to the monastery long before us but we do make it back just in time for the night rituals. Today something seems off, though. Someone is not here and it looks like everyone is worried about their white-robed friend who is not here. The routines done, we head in and to our rooms or the baths, depending on whose turn it is. Although my knowledge of their language is limited in most ways, I quickly understand that the missing monk was on his way down to the nearby village but had to turn back and is now in the recovery room. No idea how far the village is or what happened to the monk, I can't understand those complex ideas yet and, due to my rank as a red-robe, I can't just go and see the translation-able white-robe monk to ask him.

One quick bath later and back into the dormitory, one of the monks from today comes up to me and tries to explain the situation in easy terms and gestures. The white-robe monk was to go and travel down to the sister temple while another would travel up and take his place for a month. He, however, was intercepted by a runner on the way down, informing him that the monk coming up had called deathly ill and would not make it up. For this reason, there is not going to be any switches for another month. Beyond this, friendly-red-robe explains that tomorrow, a young boy from the nearby village comes up with the newspapers and other goods from the village. In exchange for these, the monks send down the items they have crafted for these to be sold. One item I have never seen the conception of but that is often mentioned and praised is a very potent tincture made from one of the lichens that grows in the caves. It's used as form of cure-all by the monks and pretty much everyone else in the area by the sound of it. Off to sleep for the night, we go and I can't believe I'm not even tired from today; it's as though the food and treatment here has allowed me a very fast recovery.

The next day, quite early a boy, not much younger than me, comes up the path and is warmly welcomed into the monastery. There are a lot of things on the sled that he has with him and, without any prompting, he hands me something too. It is a snippet from a newspaper in Chinese, or at least some language that uses their characters but, the most important part is the name written in English letters: Hayannah. It is then followed by a phone number in the United Kingdom country code. I don't want to get my hope up, this looks far too much like a play to find me but then again, this predates my arrival in the monastery and seems to be from during the time I was in the grasp of Cross-Gen. There is no reason for them to have been looking for me if they were busy torturing me at the same time. In other words, this has a small possibility of being real. On top of that, the phone number reminds me far too much of the direct line to the Rogue Mansion. I thank the young man and then am quickly found by the white-robe monk who translates the rest of the clipping for me: 'We the Rogue family and our son's partner Hayannah are looking for Falawk Iring Rogue, first human hybrid. He was kidnapped by Cross-Gen and is possibly anywhere in the world. If you have any information on him or his whereabouts, we will handsomely compensate you for those. Please call the bellow number and ask for Hayannah.' Saying that this news makes me happy is probably too much of an understatement; the fox DNA in me actually fox-yelped.

The moment everyone was told the news, now realising that there was someone looking for me out there, they immediately asked the head monk for my release so that I could go home. This is a surprisingly uncomfortable idea as my debt still doesn't seem paid back. Regardless of my thoughts on the matter, the head monk simply smiles and, with a lot of affection, pats my head between my ears. He says, 'You have my blessing and you are free of your obligations.' From that moment on, it is a frenzy of movement as all my fellow red-robe monks get things ready for my departure. The young man who brought up his sled will be taking me down to his village and then further down to the larger village down the mountain; it is only there that I can find a phone to call out from. I am told to keep my robes and given another set; local culture dictates that I am now permitted to train further and become a fully qualified monk whenever in my life I decide to. For this reason, the robes will go with me and will be a part of prised possessions.

From the head monk to the red-robes, everyone was in a mad rush to help and be kind. They prepared a bag for me with robes and some snacks for the road and got everything ready for the young man to travel back down the mountain. There is now not much left to do but saying goodbye to the people who saved my life and then we are off.

With few words but a lot of gestures, the young man explains that on the way down we ride the sled but that it goes very fast so I must hold on to it. If you are wondering, I was never told his name and never learnt the correct vocabulary to ask for it. When I gestured the typical 'me Falawk, you ??' He just looked puzzled and kept going. We are now mounting his sled, my legs up at the front, him steering from the back. The moment we kick off down the slope, I realise why he said I have to hold on. We are not going down the walking path but rather down a much more direct line which slops a lot more. Quickly the whiteness around us becomes a blur – with nothing to judge speed from – I can only guess how fast we are going, too fast for health insurance to cover your injuries. Making a few turns, we slow down at the sight of a few houses and, not in the softest way possible, come to a halt between the ten or so buildings that are here. We dismount, are rapidly greeted and ushered into a large building. There, in very few words, the sled man explains the situation and who I am. They all seem to have known about my existence anyway as no one is particularly surprised by the ears and tail, eyes or fur.

After what seemed to be barely a few minutes, we are off again. Some produce from the sled traded with the people here, some more things gathered up. We need to make haste; the sun sets in an hour and, I am told, the ride down takes time even in the best weather conditions. Kicking off again, the terrifying vehicle gets up to a crazy speed just as fast as before. The only difference is that, this time, there are rocks to avoid and other obstacles that need to be swerved around and that prevent my mind from figuring out our speed. The answer to said speed is a lot. We are going very fast and I really hope that sled-man knows how to drive this thing like a formula one race driver. He does have great skill in steering us around boulders long before they could cause a problem. He makes us narrowly avoid two cliffs that were trying to serve as deadly speed bumps. In more ways than one, this is the fondest experience I've had in many moons and it is certainly one worth living regardless of the fear it generates. There are far too many good reasons for this to go wrong and yet thanks to, what must be, years of experience, the town is in sight just as the sun sinks behind the tallest snowy peak.

With the town in sight, super-sled driver somehow manages to slow us down, using a rope and a stick, so that we don't crash into the buildings. Again, he parks us in the middle of the town and we are immediately greeted by happy childish squeals. It would seem he has a daughter or a younger sibling as she is hopping towards us and jumps into his arms before even letting him get off the sled. He picks her up and, in the dialect of the temple tells me she is his daughter. So, he is a lot older than I thought or he had his child quite early. In the ways of the monks who taught me so well, I greet the child with all the courtesy needed for a first meeting. She is so surprised when I appear out from behind her brother that she actually lets out a little scream. I step back and bow to which she immediately responds in kind. Apparently, the bow is the best greeting to use and that will be my technique for all the following encounters. The young girl skips over to me and asks to touch my tail; I let her despite the cringe it causes and the tickles.

While the encounter with the sweet little girl is lovely, the village chief is now here. We all help unload the sled; soon I am ushered into the largest building in the village. It serves as a meeting hall and an emergency shelter in case of extreme weather. Not only is this village the nearest the temple that has a telephone, I was immediately taken to said telephone in this large one-room building. Before I am asked anything, the newspaper is produced and the number dialled in.

'Hello, you have reached Rogue Mansion, if you are calling in regards to the disappearance of Falawk Iring Rogue, please stay on the line, if not, please renew your call at a later stage.' A long silence and then 'Hello, this is Hayannah, whom am I speaking to' I can't believe my ears. The accent, the tone, everything, it's really her and she is in Scotland at the mansion.

— 'Hello Hayannah, could you please record this for proof for my father?' I ask without remembering to first say who I am. I doubt she can guess.
— 'All these calls are recorded sir, but why your father, we don't share the recordings?
— —It's me Hayannah, I'm alive, in a village in the Himalayas and I want to go home.' I manage to blurt out before I can stop myself. The tears run down my fury cheeks and soon I'm plain crying.
— 'Falawk, if that's really you, I need you to certify it and tell me where you are in more details.' Says a slightly faltering voice I recognise as my little sister Leyna.
— 'Leyna, n'ei lé virk en ta huüs karn'naa'ak vèïlk. I'm alive and well. It's a long story but I don't know how you're going to get to where I am. I'm in a village in the Himalayas and not entirely sure where.' I can't add anything more before I hear my father's voice.

— 'We are on our way; we managed to trace the call and know where you are. We'll be there as soon as humanly possible. Please stay safe son.' And, to my surprise, he then hangs up the call.

Trying to explain that my family found me without me even knowing where I am, that they are on their way and that I'll be leaving within a week at most, well those are all difficult to explain to someone you have just met. This is even more challenging when you are speaking a language of which you only dabble in the basics of. Thankfully, the head of the village is perfectly alright with the guest of the temple staying in his little town. This means that, until my family make it here, I'll have a place to stay and I'll even get food; two things I could never repay them enough for.

The sheer shock of finding out that Hayannah is still alive comes as a crashing wave of emotions as soon as my hosts left me alone in what is to be my room for the next days, while I wait. After the, supposedly fake video I was shown at Cross-Gen, I thought that I had caused her death and that, on top of everything else, if I ever survived and got free, another sad trip to Korea would be needed. There is little to nothing I can now do while waiting for my family to magically appear in this tiny village lost in the mountains and come and pick me up.

Travelling Again

Falling asleep is easy for the first time in a long time. Not only are the warm earthen coloured walls comforting, the soft crackle of the fire, the piles of blankets under and on top me, and the silence of the night all help to cradle me to sleep. A dreamless sleep takes over and, before long, I am being woke by a loud commotion in the village. Someone runs in and calls out to me saying something to the essence of 'The travellers have made their way up through the valley' which means there are people arriving in the village. Seeing as how the monks at the temple made a huge deal about anyone arriving there, I can but guess that this is the same sort of situation.

Donning my robe as fast as I can, I dash out of the room, through the large hall and then straight into the main plaza area. With the sun high in the sky, it must be long past midday, I can now see that this village is in fact not so small as I thought. That is, however, not the most remarkable factor, all the houses are painted with a great deal of intricate designs in many different colours. This creates a kaleidoscope of hues and tones all around the plaza giving it a vibrantly glowing ambiance against the ever-present snow. The day must be very clear because the small halfway village and the temple are both visible up on the mountain. Seeing as how high they are on the mountain, either they are very close to the peaks or we travelled much further than I thought yesterday afternoon. Looking at how steep and barren the slopes are, it's a wonder we are still alive, sled man and myself.

That aside, there is not a sound in the town but everyone seems to be listening out for something far away in utter quietness. Without thinking, my overly sensitive ears pick up on engine noises coming up the mountain at good speed. I barely noticed it but there really is a road leading all the way to this village up in the mountains. It's crazy to think that they would bother doing that kind of construction work when it's doubtful that anyone is even able to drive up here or owns a car. The noise tells me that the vehicles being used are not your average cars but rather military grade trucks and four by fours. My instincts tell me to hide before the village leader tells me to do so. He tells me I should hide in the room in case these people are not the ones I am hoping for but rather the people who captured me previously. Logically, they could be my family but that would mean that they travelled here ridiculously fast. It can't have been more than fifteen hours since I called them.

Hiding away in my room, I keep my ears wide open and listen for the moment the vehicles stop at the entrance of the village and end of the road. Things seem to just stop at that point. Brakes squeal, tyres skid a little and motors are turned off. Then I hear a door open and slam shut, and another and then many more. Footsteps run into the village and only stop a few seconds before getting louder and louder. The person is running to my room at ridiculous speed. It's only been ten steps when the door crashes open and something flies at me.

Instincts take over and I pull the flying thing into a violent martial art movement flipping her onto the floor and pinning her down. Wait her? She smells familiar. The adrenaline is still flowing too much for me to be able to tell what is going on but things are rapidly cleared up.

— 'Falawk, it's me. It's Hayannah. You're not in danger any more, you don't need to fight back so much.' Says the girl on the floor. She really is Hayannah. I immediately get off her and go to help her up but she pulls me down on top of her and kisses me. 'You have no idea how long I've waited to do that again.

— How are you still alive? I mean, I know I heard your voice on the phone but ... they showed me footage of how they killed you in the airport.' I hear more footsteps and then Leyna bursts into the room and jumps onto the two of us without a care in the world.

— 'I missed you! I can't believe this had to happen again. I'm never leaving your side again big bro.' She says between tears. I think the only reason my tears are yet to flow like the great Han River is purely due to shock.

— 'I missed you too little sis. Should we get up? I hear Dad coming.' Only as I get up do I see that something major has changed. 'Hayannah, Leyna, since when are you two hybrids? I know you were in the process of becoming one Leyna but you Hayannah? I think we have a lot of catching up to do.' I ask them. We get up and, before they have time to reply, Dad walks in with a rather official looking military man and the village leader.

— 'My son, I thought I would never see you again. I don't even have words for how I feel right now.' He just starts crying and then so do I. We all end up crying awkwardly as mister-military-man and the village chief watch us.

To not bore you too much, let me just say this: when you are believed dead and you have been feeling left alone and abandoned for a long time, it's quite difficult to process your emotions. This is even more true when you find out that what you thought was months was a full year. The hybridisation of Hayannah and Leyna should be enough to tell me that but it was still a huge shock when Dad said it had been thirteen months since I disappeared from Incheon airport. Now on our back home, Dad has been on the phone – using a satellite phone – the entire trip down the mountain. He has been speaking in English, French, Chinese and a few other languages I didn't know he had learnt nor can I recognise them.

With Dad up front, I'm sitting in the back of the off-road truck with my sister on one side and Hayannah on the other. I keep wanting to say that she is my girlfriend but then that just doesn't feel right. We barely had a few days to get to know each other before thirteen months and a week went past before we saw each other again. The kiss she left on my lips should have told me how she felt but I'm still confused. Leyna is typing away on her tablet while nuzzling herself again me regardless of the bumps on the road. Hayannah seems to be in a daze, I think she is feeling a little motion sick too.

The trip down the mountain goes a lot faster than I thought; probably something to do with the vehicles being adapted to this sort of madness. The driver must be going nearly ninety kilometres per hour down these freshly ploughed bends and turns. Right at the front is an off-road snow plough that is clearing snow and salting the road for us. Once we got to a plateau area, they drive us to a small airport where a set of military double propellor helicopters are waiting for us. We drive right into the back of them and are told we can either wait in the car or get out. Hayannah not being at her best, she wants to stay here so we all do. Take off is nice and smooth but rather noise – between us hybrids' overly sensitive hearing and a lack of soundproofing – it almost hurts. Leyna hands out modified noise-cancelling earbuds that immediately help a lot. Hayannah needed a little help getting hers in, she is not used to her hybrid ears' position just yet and gets confused about it quite often by the seeing of it.

Landing about an hour later jolts me awake. I fell asleep – balled up against Hayannah – without even realising it. She doesn't seem to mind so much as I can clearly see the line left by a drop of her drool down my red robe. Gently waking her up when they drive us back out of the helicopter and across a tarmac to an airport terminal. It just dawned on me that going through customs might be a little complicated for me considering I don't have a passport with me. Once in the airport, Dad finally gets off his fiftieth call and actually talks to us.

— 'Alright, because of the international ramifications of Falawk's reappearance, we are being required to talk to media as soon as we make it back to the UK. I've negotiated for it to be a BBC exclusive on normal TV rather than a press conference. It will be simultaneously retransmitted and translated across the world.' Starts dad making me wonder who on earth he was talking to for that long.
— 'Do you mean that they see me as important to that extent? That's a little strange.' If you think about it, sure I'm the first hybrid but that should not warrant the entire world's media to care about me.
— 'You are not just the first hybrid Falawk, your blood is the key to hybridisation and it's now been copied by Cross-Gen. They released an article on the deep web stating there will be an auction for the key.

— They are going to auction off my blood? That's messed up even for them.

— Not your blood, a highly effective hybridisation cocktail that can create super soldiers.

— Ah, now it makes sense why everyone wants to know the source of their future nightmares.' I'm still reeling from the emotions of seeing my family again and now I have to deal with those crazy scientists creating living weapons because of me.

— 'Actually, big bro, people want to hear what happened to you while you were gone and they also want your insight on hybrids. As the first one in the world, you are the only "expert" per se'. Says Leyna. She has been working on something none-stop on her tablet thing and only now do I see what it is.

— 'Are you busy designing a plane? Why?' She is amazing, but to design an entire aeroplane, she has clearly been studying this past year.

— 'It's going to be our new vehicle. My patents for the motors and fuel systems have already been accepted. Back on topic, we will need to get on top of our guest list dad. There are going to be a lot of demands to meet Falawk and I think we need to delay them all by at least a month.

— Way ahead of you Leyna, I've got everyone scheduled in a month's time and have set up neutral meeting grounds for the political meetings.' Replies Hayannah. I didn't even realise this until now but she has picked up a little of the family accent in her English. Probably a side effect living with them long enough of that to happen.

— 'Again, I'll have a lot to catch up on in the next days to be sure I'm up to date on what's going on.' And that's all truer when I realise that dad has a passport for me in hand and we are being ushered to a private jet.

We board the plane and immediately things become a little calmer. Firstly, we are flying directly to Heathrow London and the flight will take a full eight hours. That gives us all time to work on preparations and rest. Hayannah and I are sitting together in a little cubicle sort of space, over the wings for extra comfort. We have laptops and tablets out trying to write down as much critical information about the happenings of the last year. This gives me a great opportunity to catch up on things that were happening at home and that I missed out on.

Firstly, right after my disappearance, Hayannah requested to switch all her classes online and pretty much ran away from home to go to Scotland and help in the search. Dad not being a huge fan of this, he invited her parents and they had a long chat about her taking responsibility for her actions. That's apparently when my dad just wrote her a full-time job contract and a hefty salary; that cleared the air rapidly and allowed Hayannah to stay and live the way she wanted to. About a month into her moving there, Hayannah was able to experience the painless version of a hybridisation process as

Leyna had hers done using the key extracted from my blood. Dad had managed to come to the conclusion that it was a specific part of my blood that served as the key. It's not even a problem if I'm of a different blood group to the person receiving it, the key still works. It took about three weeks for the first major changes to appear on my sister and that's when Hayannah decided to go through with the process too. She justified it simply by saying that it will give her a better chance in life and will allow her to do a lot more than a normal person. She then chose a lot of the same DNA as mine and Leyna's but also added the breathing capability of whales. This somehow made her blood oxygenation a lot more efficient and she can hold her breath for nearly half an hour while still moving around. Her full hybridisation only completed about a month and a half ago and thankfully she is loving each second of it.

We keep going over the events of the past year but it's mainly focussed on me retelling all I remember of the Cross-Gen centre and then the temple. We rapidly realised that there was a lot more done to me than that which I can remember. Mostly because of a lot of scar tissue I can't remember the source of but also from the huge memory gaps between events. Sure, they used a lot of drugs on me but I think it was a game to them rather than an actual desire to extract information out of me. Surely, after trying for months on end, and then finding the answer themselves, they must have realised how little I knew of what they were asking me. I knew my blood could do something as Dad used it for Leyna but I didn't consciously know it was the key. I wonder if they got that information out of me.

It takes us a good two hours to catch up on all of my things; Hayannah is especially interested in the temple stay and the things I learnt there. In her words 'It's an amazingly rare opportunity' and I should really cherish those memories. Although I find this somewhat entertaining, considering the amount of pain I was in upon arrival, there is no reason for not to remember people being so kind to me. That piece of advice brings our conversation to an end and laptops and tablets are put away. As we do, I see Leyna balled up on her seat fast asleep. Dad is still typing away and he seems to not be anywhere near done. Hayannah smiles at me and pushes her chair into bed mode. She then invites me to do the same and our bed-chairs meet to form a sort of double bed. She closes the curtain on the side, pats the bed and just says, 'It's safe to rest.'

A New Life

London

When I wake up, it's sometime in the early morning and our pilot is calling for us to put our seats up as we will be landing in Heathrow soon. A car is already waiting there to take us to the BBC offices in the centre. Due to us arriving in a private plane, the entire customs process is pre-cleared and we'll have little to nothing to do.

Landing happens without so much as a bump and soon we are taxiing off to the private hangers. There, we are met by two, very official looking, secret service officers. They say little but check our passports, stamp them and simply say 'welcome home' before inspecting the plane. Dad tells me that, because of where we came from, there is a pretty high risk of having a stowaway so they have to check. We walk across the tarmac to a waiting van that I immediately recognise as one of dad's modified cars. There is no driver so I can only guess that, either it drove itself here or they left it here before coming to get me.

Getting in, the vehicle seems a little different and dad immediately points it out to me: there is a whole in all the seats for a tail to fit through. On top of that, all the windows are bullet-proof glass and so is the rest of the vehicle. It may look like an ordinary minivan but it's actually a two-ton tank undercover. A voice command in the family language, given in a quick and direct voice, get the silent vehicle to start up and take us forth. Using only highly sophisticated electrical motors, this beast of a van moves smoothly and quietly. We are soon avoiding cars and weaving through traffic as we make it to the centre of the capital.

Arriving at the BBC headquarters, a huge and quite imposing building, we are ushered into an underground parking lot. Here, we are met by two burly security guards who seem extra weary of us three hybrids, not because of our appearance but because they must feel our overwhelming strength. These people clearly know their jobs well. They badge us into a lift and soon we shoot up to the thirty-fifth floor. Outside the lift's doors, a very excited looking reporter is waiting and we are soon guided to a preparation room. In order not to leak any information to the greater public, they plan on interrupting their evening program for our interview. This both helps with security and competition trying to interfere with the broadcast.

We are rapidly pampered for the camera, mainly just offered a nice hair and fur brush for us three hybrids. They want us looking as natural as possible, according to them. This works great for me as I really don't feel like being touched in any way by people I don't know. Not after the far too recent events.

As soon as we're ready to go, things escalate.

— 'Dear viewers, we are interrupting our evening program with some breaking news. Just arriving back on British ground minutes ago, Falawk Iring Rogue, first human hybrid, has made it home after a year in captivity. His family, girlfriend and he are here this evening to tell you all what happened and how things went down for him to make it back.' That's our queue to get in front of the camera, the green screen behind us is being used to project images of us under other angles. 'Welcome to you all, thank you for coming here so soon after getting back. I'm sure everyone is tired so we'll keep this to the main details. Could you all please introduce yourselves.

— 'Hello everyone, I am Doctor Pieter Rogue, original co-creator of the human hybridisation theory alongside my late wife.' Starts dad. For once he is bothering to use his full name and not just his title as he usually does.

— 'Hello, I am Hayannah Kim. I am an employee of Rogue Incorporated and third successful human hybrid worldwide.

— Hello, I am Leyna Rogue, doctor of genetic and molecular biology, Sister to Falawk, Daughter to Doctor Rogue and second human hybrid.' That's my little sister, casually telling the whole world she has a double PhD at her far too young age.

— 'Greetings to you all, I am Falawk Iring Rogue, first hybrid.' I leave it at that, not really knowing what else I should add. All things considered, that is a decent introduction.

— 'Thank you. So, I'm going to start by asking the obvious question: Falawk, what happened to you?' This is going to be interesting.

— 'Would you like the full story or should I sensor some of the gritty details for your viewers?

— I would love the full story but for now, could you sensor it and give us the major events.

— Of course.' And so, I run through the events. Starting from Cross-Gen assassinating Byeol-I and my trip to Korea to visit her parents and offer my condolences. From this all the way to the phone call that got me home. I leave out some of the more personal details and especially avoid detailing the tortures and the treatment from Cross-Gen.

— 'Thank you for keeping that brief but detailed. Hayannah, I believe you had a large part to play in finding Falawk. I also want to ask about your hybridisation. Could you tell us more about those?' They are really giving us a lot of freedom to speak our minds and say only what we want to.

— 'After Falawk got kidnapped in front of my eyes, I immediately called Leyna who was my point of contact and I told her everything that had happened. Feeling responsible in some absurd way, I decided to request my courses be taken online and asked Doctor Rogue if I could move to their house to help look for his son. They allowed me to. It is during that time – as I was helping them with far more than just looking for Falawk – that the offer to become a hybrid came and was accepted. The changes took quite some time but I'm really happy with how things turned out. As for finding Falawk, well, he actually found us. He simply called the number I was monitoring and thus we found his location, went there as fast as possible and brought him back.' She blows past what feels like a lot of critical details but then again, we probably shouldn't really tell the entire world everything about our private lives.

— 'Waou, that must really have been an intense time. I'm sure you're expecting everyone to ask you this so let me beat the tabloids to it: Are you two dating?' Now that's a question I don't know the answer for myself.

— 'Of course. I don't think I could have had the energy to pull off a year-long search for him if it were not for love. He was the first person I fell in love with and I was not about to lose that.' Oh.

— 'I see Falawk is blushing. I guess you two have not really had time to catch up. Sorry for the personal question about your relationship. I'm just glad you two are finally reunited. Now, if Leyna and Doctor Rogue would like to give a few of their details?'

The interview doesn't drag on much longer and, soon, we are walking off the stage and are taken a few floors up to the offices of the presenters. Here they have a little snack set out for us and I'm asked for a recorded version of the Cross-Gen torture and other related events. They will be sending it off to Interpol and the secret services so that it can be used in the track for Cross-Gen members. I also take this time to ask them to send out word that Jenny is still missing.

With that all done and dusted, we are to head back to the van when the two security guards from earlier come up to get us. Apparently, there is a rather large swarm of people, especially hybrid fans and tabloid journalists, swarming outside. They get us back to the van, somehow managing to clear the crowd away and let us through. Encouragingly, I spot quite a lot of smiles and waves in the crowd rather than anything else. This is a welcome sight considering everything that has been going on.

With the van on autopilot, Dad finally takes some rest. Leyna takes first watch so that the rest of us can sleep more too. Not much needs doing as the van can get us home on one tank so we just take turns monitoring. Hayannah, having now told the country and, subsequently, the world, that she is my girlfriend, decided to use my lap as a cushion. Just as I'm looking forward, to the road, Leyna winks at me, looks away and then Hayannah pulls my head down into a very soft and fond kiss.

At Last

Making it home that night is probably one of the most ecstatic feelings I've had in a long time. My family finding me was crazy, that kiss earlier was amazing, this is plain bliss. Finally, regardless of what I may fear, I am finally safe and can actually relax for a little while.

With a series of voice commands, Hayannah gets the bath to start heating up as we head up to our rooms. I'm still in my room but she has now joined it too. Leyna decided to give us a few days even if she really wants to spend time with me. As we're all really tired, this quickly turned into a 'let's just hit the baths together and call it a night'. Being both a girl and a boy physically does make it a little awkward in some regards but then again, thanks to some new ability my hybrid brain developed, I have very good control over what my reactions to things are. For various reasons, dad requests that we all head to the labs first.

— 'I'm sorry to ask you all three to do this but I can't risk ever losing you in any way again.' He says before sitting us down and asking us to drop our tops to expose our backs.
— 'Big bro, they really did a number on you, your back is covered in scars. I can see them even through you fur.' It's

true that there was never a dull moment in the last few years.

— 'Even with the awesome healing abilities I gained from becoming a hybrid, there is still the issue of scar tissue. I doubt that will ever go away sadly. I hope you don't mind Hayannah?

— Of course, I don't. It's a part of you now, as sad as that is. I just hope you don't ever have to get any more.' We are still waiting for Dad to finish his tinkering on the computers. He comes over with an injection gun in his hand. This makes me flinch far more than I would like.

— 'Don't worry you three, this is a new form of tracker that lightly alters your infrared signature to make it easy to find on satellite. It's not a chip so it can't be removed. Also, Falawk, we need to talk about your hybridisation.

— Why so dad? Is there something wrong with me?

— On the contrary, Leyna and myself have found that you have a very specific gene that should make you a very good leader to other hybrids. You have an Alpha gene.

He then goes on to explain that I can, should I wish to, give commands and infuse them with a kind of pheromone that will make all hybrids listen and react to what I say. This can't work on Leyna or Hayannah though as both of them also have the gene. He managed to replicate it after looking into my blood more in depth. The injections take less than a second each and we are then finally off to the baths.

Hayannah at my side, we are ridiculously awkward owing to the fact that she openly proclaimed herself my girlfriend yet we only ever kissed three times. It's all the more difficult with Leyna constantly edging us on with silly jokes. She really is fond of my tomato face it would seem. Regardless of my shyness, the girl part of me is struggling with hormones at the moment and that really doesn't help with my feelings. There is not much other to do than get into the baths, soak, relax and enjoy.

Our furs glistening with beads of condensed steam, tails wagging in the water, the three of us just relish in our time and talk about further plans. Although Leyna already has doctorates, she really wants to at least go to university for a year or two and experience that kind of life. Hayannah would like to do a master's degree in intercultural relations and write a thesis on hybrid-human community living. She recons this is something that will be interesting and that she is currently the most qualified person to research. As for myself, I think getting in-person degrees and furthering my education as originally planned would be nice. The conversation lingers on and rapidly turns into a debate about locations. Hayannah wants to experience France and thus thinks that studying there would be fun but I'm less convinced considering my time there previously was not the best. Leyna wants only the best of the best and thus aims for the universities in the USA, especially MIT and Caltech. She quickly convinces Hayannah and me that going to North America would be fun. That's when the idea of Quebec comes up. It's a French-speaking area but it's also in North America and not ridiculously far from MIT.

Bathed and clean, we head to bed and, without a word said between them, Hayannah helps Leyna bring her pillows, duvet and teddy to my bed. Apparently, regardless of my opinion, we are all sleeping together tonight. That's going to be nice. Nice to finally be safe and be able to rest comfortably with the people I love surrounding me. We fall asleep comfortably snuggled against each other. It was rapidly clear that, with three fury hybrids in a bed, blankets are really optional extras, so we settled for only using one large one wrapped over all of us.

The next morning, or afternoon, it's a little unclear, I wake up alone in bed with a little not on the nightstand saying, 'Sleepyhead, breakfast is ready.' I quickly go and deal with my girl business, in other words, cleaning a diva cup, these things are a little difficult to get used to but they are magical. Once that's done, it's time to choose an outfit – a fresh tunic robe seems the most adequate at this point so that's what I look for. Turns out, the only thing I have like that is my spare red robes from the temple so that's not going to do. Settling for a skirt and long sleeve jumper, I head down to breakfast only to find the dining room and kitchen area totally empty. Another note says 'eat up, we're outside' so I find a plank of food and – sorting through the things – find some rice, fruit and a little bit of dried mushrooms. There is a bunch of meat and eggs but I really don't feel like cooking stuff that requires oil. The temple time and more importantly, albeit less nice, the Cross-Gen time, got me a little weary of hot oil or fatty foods.

As soon as I'm done with my meal, the instructions quite clear, I head outside and go look for everyone. It's pretty easy to find them in the forest as they are being rather loud. Leyna and Hayannah are running through a course of obstacles and weights and other things while Dad watches them and gives advice. When he sees me, he simply says I should watch as he'll want to send me through the course in a few minutes. This is apparently a daily routine: Get up, eat breakfast, train for an hour, start the day. I quickly see that the obstacles are hybrid only as there are ten-meter jumps and tight-rope balancing sections which no human could complete. There is also a rather frightful high to this entire thing which really doesn't make me feel too confident.

The girls finish up and jump down, landing in a very fluid motion, tucked into a roll. They get up and give me each a nice sweaty hug. Only then do I see that they are both wearing only sports underwear. It's quite cold out – probably snow temperature – and yet neither of them is shivering as we hybrids produce a lot of heat. Hayannah then just wishes me luck as it's my turn. I take off my skirt and top and am thus only wearing nice and tight undies. To get up to the course one must jump and, to my astonishment, it's an easy jump although I know it's far beyond anything human. Dad then runs me through the obstacles and what I must do before starting a timer.

I run, jump, climb, drop, roll, balance and swing along all the obstacles as fast as possible. It's a really fun feeling but I can clearly see how it would become tiring if I have to do it many times in a row. The obstacles are made mostly of logs and are thus also a little slippery which really doesn't help things when it comes to jumps requiring precision. The training regimen is quite severe but the most complicated part of it is not the layout of the course or even the general difficulty, it's that endurance is the key to doing it fully. The girls have run through it five times by the time I complete my first run. Not only are they able to complete it fast but even add extra difficulty by springing from one obstacle to the next backwards or with flips and other madness. That being said, it is ridiculously fun and soon makes me wish I was far more in shape.

Dad then has us take ten laps around the property before we all head to a sauna I didn't know was in the house. Leyna says it's new and the they added it especially for post-training relaxation. This is, by a long shot, the most intense training I've ever heard of. We are sitting in the sauna, sweating off and throwing ice cold water onto the steaming hot stones in the middle while discussing our next move. It would seem sleeping in makes you miss a lot of interesting discussions in this house. Hayannah and dad had a long chat about studying and came to the conclusion that Quebec and MIT would both be interesting as would Vancouver and Seattle. This led to a full-on debate about where is best to stay considering the costs of studies and so on to which dad apparently said, 'They owe me favours in three of those places so I'll figure it out when you guys have decided what to do.' From there on out, Leyna joined in and they had time to run a few different scenarios before deciding to go with MIT and Montreal as it's easy to fly between them. With Leyna working on a new kind of jet engine that runs on hydrogen – Dad having developed an incredibly efficient electrolysis device that can extract hydrogen from any water given to it – and there being a few very well-funded rocket labs near and at MIT, they have high hopes.

As soon as we are showered off, this time separately, we head in and the discussion picks up where it left off.

— 'So, when would you three like to register? You could go as early as next month and entre in the winter semester or you could wait for September.' Asks Dad pulling up a holographic display, another one of the family's recent inventions and patents.

— 'I think we can all agree that the sooner the better so let's aim for this January's intake. I don't think it's going to be difficult for us to get in, it's more a question of getting there and getting set up.' Responds Leyna to which Hayannah and I nod in agreement.

— 'Setting you up will be quite easy, the critical thing now is just to figure out safety and logistics of getting there, making sure you are all three equipped for any possible interactions with Cross-Gen and other outside forces, as well as making sure you all know what you want to study.

— I'm going to pursue electrical engineering and computer programming for now with a bit of extra time spent in political science to work on international relations.' I've been thinking about it for a while already and this does seem like the best option for now. I'm going to have to start from the bottom and work my way up but I should manage to negotiate my way out of a lot of credits if I can pass higher-level classes.

— 'I'll be doing intercultural studies and graphic design as I love those things. Probably, depending on how things go, I'll also pick up French just to help in the future.' Adds Hayannah.

— 'And I'll be doing a triple post-doctorate in aeronautics, biology and international law. There's no way they'll allow me to do more than that at once anyway so it'll have to be enough for now.' Leyna casual reminding us all that she is already a PhD in far too many fields before I even had time to study a normal bachelor's degree.

— 'Alright, I'll get you interviews lined up for registration. It's a little close notice but I'm sure some strings can be pulled. Leyna, I'll use one of your patents as a door for you. Hayannah, your previous degree is so darned good that you'll get in easily and Falawk, well, you'll have to do it the hard way again, sorry son.

— It's fine, that seems to be the way for everything in my life so it's becoming more of a habit than a shock. Can you get Hayannah and me into the universities in Montreal? That would be ideal for French, I think.

— Sure thing, I'll make sure this all works out. We'll all travel together to get you two settled in and then I'll take Leyna to Boston and move her in too.'

We keep preparing plans and sharing our ideas for the next few days. This leads to my interview with a very excited pedagogical supervisor who recons I can skip straight to the last year and graduate in one semester because of my prior knowledge and learning speed. I'll have to take 45 credit hours per week though but that's not a problem. Leyna didn't just get in, they actually invited her as soon as Dad called the head office asking if there was a possibility – apparently, because of her new jet propulsion system patent – she is rather famous in that field. According to the lab there, they can have a functioning prototype of her jet built within less than a month if she'll give them access to the patent. Hayannah also had an interview and, to our collective surprise, it was held in Korean. The head of the languages department happens to be married to a Korean national so they speak the language fluently. With most of everything sorted out, we are getting ready to move out and go to Canada as a first ever trip together. Dad got himself roped into speaking at twelve different conferences but this is also what allowed the three of us hybrids to be easily accepted into our respective campuses.

When it came to housing, Dad said the solution he found Hayannah and I is a secret. Leyna is getting a penthouse apartment which he bought on auction for a pittance. It does need some fixing up but she is more than happy to deal with that and dad will help her between conferences. Beyond those things, we are nearly ready to go and dad got us onto an empty-leg flight on a private jet again for less than £300 for all of us. There are always ways of doing expensive things for cheap according to him and he really is good at showing that off. The one condition he had for all of us is that he is going to have us install a full security system in each of our places and then code it to link to the main house. For such an installation to happen, we need to take with and order a lot of materials otherwise it would be impossible to set up in a timely manner.

Moving in and Studies

The day of the flight comes so much faster than I thought and we are off to a small private airport near the

Scottish capital. The van is packed full of gear, suitcases and other needed items for work, research and just living too. The drive is a quick one; before we know it, we are pulling up to the security office and showing our passports. The guy there greets Dad like an acquaintance and lets us in. From entering the airport until boarding takes barely a few minutes. We go through a very rapid security check, have our passports stamped and then we're off to board. The pilot greets us very kindly and says we can be in the air as soon as everything is loaded as the plane is already fuelled up. We'll be flying directly to Montreal and don't have to make any stops on the way so it's a good time to take a long nap or play games or something.

Take-off is smooth and, faster than I thought, the captain tells us that autopilot is on and we can now relax for the rest of the trip. Food is the first thing we have after reaching cruising altitude. From there, it's mostly card games, a few rounds of table tennis and a few movies. Leyna and Hayannah have got close over the past year, so they keep ganging up on me. Since I've been back, Hayannah has been quite shy around me even if we share a room and a bed. It's not easy to get into the mindset of being a couple after so long apart from each other. There is also the fact that I don't really know how to lead and neither does she so we keep kissing and then looking at each other awkwardly. It's fun but leads to a rather profound frustration as we are seeking more but have no idea what to do about it. After our food and games, the girls are having fun with my tail fur, braiding it into different patterns. Because I can't really jump away from them, I just leave them to it but the tickling is horrendous.

At some point, the three of us fell asleep in a pile on the floor and someone put blankets over us which is really thoughtful but now I'm dying of heat. Hybrids produce a lot of heat, that's one thing, the other thing is that we are not the most peaceful sleepers. I wake up with Hayannah drooling on my tummy and Leyna hugging my tail. It's impossible to move but also really uncomfortable so I just wiggle until they let go. That leaves me just enough clearance to get up and go and look out the window and see the snow below as we are flying over Canada already. I wake the girls up, a hug for Leyna and a lingering kiss for my girlfriend. Oh, I just said that word. Well, I guess my mind is dealing with it a lot better than I thought.

With their permission, I went and watched the landing from the cockpit and the pilots even let me 'feel' the landing by siting in co-pilot. This just gave me a burning desire to get my licence so that I can fly too. It's a kind of fun I didn't know existed but that I want to repeat now. Once touched down, we taxi to a private hanger and from there get a bus to the terminal and go through incoming customs. Somehow, because we are students, they let us through with very little questions although one of the security agents asks for a picture with the three first ever hybrids. One smile and a flash later, we are off to the rental agency to pick up a van and go back to the hangar to get all our stuff. This was the easiest way of doing things and leads to a much faster arrival process according to the pilots.

Finally, on our way into the city, Dad tells us that we'll both need to get our licences converted as we can't drive on foreign ones for more than three months. Hayannah asks why we would need to drive and he simply says that it will make our life easier. The surprise he has is starting to seem a lot bigger than I would like for it to be but that's beyond our control, he is far too proud of whatever he set up. We drive for a little while, past the university and then off to the west of it. From here, it's around a few bends and then onto a much older-looking street. The houses here are visibly from the last century. Saying that, they look very comfortable and as Dad is slowing down, I guess this is the surprise.

— 'I think you can guess that one of these is your future home. Now, to not spoil anything, I'm going to give you the keys and you'll need to find the right one.' Says dad handing Hayannah a key card and then tapping one to a new wristband and handing it to me.
— 'So, we just need to find the house with a card reader on the front gate and that's home? Should be easy enough.
— Who said it would be a house and who said it would be on a gate Falawk. The only hint I'll give you is that the entrance is on this street.

— Somewhere on the street, are you saying it could be in a wall?

— No more hints.' He smiles and sits back into the car. Leyna somehow produced a bag of popcorn and is watching Hayannah and I with that obnoxious face of 'I know the answer but won't tell you.'

We end up spending a good half hour discreetly going to each house and looking for something to tap the cards against but to no avail. I just started searching up and down the walls on the other side of the road; it has houses on one side and a terraced hill on the other. The hill is well overgrown and looks like a park of some sort. Hayannah is coming towards me from further up the street with a triumphant smile. 'I found it,' she tells me and guides me to an ajar opening in the terrace wall. We call Dad and Leyna who are deep in discussion and tell them we found the entrance but I have no idea to what it leads.

Dad smiles at us and pushes the door/stone, inward fully. Behind it is a rather murky looking tunnel that is badly lit by a few dirty bulbs and the filtered in sunlight from the opening. He tells us to walk straight down and up the stairs at the end; he'll be driving around with the van. It's lovely how he makes us go in the murky way while he can go around through the front gate. It does have a suspenseful feeling to it, coming through this passageway and up the stairs. At the top of the stairs, a lightly ornate door waits for us and it also opens with the key cards. This time we use my wristband to make sure it works; it does perfectly. Clicking and swinging open, the door reveals a large room with stairs off to the left, two huge floor-to-ceiling windows and what can only be the front door. Opposite from the windows and between this door and the main door, a wood fireplace awaits a nice warm fire later. The rest of the place is rather bare which calls for a little shopping spree later. We hear Dad stopping in front of the main door and open up for Leyna and him to enter.

— 'So, what do you think of the little secret entrance to your new house? It was such a strange feature that no one wanted to buy this place. You should see how long it was on the market for. I had to have a cleaning crew here for a full week to get it ready for you two.
— That's really kind of you daddy Rogue.' That's what Hayannah calls dad. 'Can we explore the rest of the place?
— Of course, that's the whole idea. I'm going to set up a few of the security features while you choose a room for yourselves and then we can discuss furniture and other needed things.
— Can I come with you two lovebirds?' Asks Leyna with a silly voice.
— 'Nope, you have to stay here.' I say jokingly before pulling her along at a run towards the stairs.

It's a little strange but that huge room on the ground floor is the only room there, everything else starts on the second floor. We find a stripped bare kitchen, a dining room and a small bathroom. One floor up there are three bedrooms and a larger bathroom and finally, right at the top, there is a really big bedroom and an on-suite bathroom. The roof slants down here giving it a sort of circular dome feeling and, at the top of said roof is an actual glass dome. There are also four shuttered windows that see out to all directions once opened. Hayannah doesn't need to ask, this is going to be the master bedroom and thus our new nest. It feels huge as there is no furniture and the walls even are bare. Leyna chooses a room on the second floor as we go down and calls it her 'spare nest'. We head down to the kitchen area and find Dad there busy taking pictures on his tablet, thus measuring things up. He is apparently done setting up a rudimentary security system for the place which includes a few motion detectors, cameras, infrared signature recognition systems and a few other bits.

Once we are done emptying the van of Hayannah and my things, we drop off dad's and Leyna's in the entrance room and head out to HKea to get furniture for the entire place. With this being North America, we can have everything delivered and installed before the end of the week. The only thing we need to do before then is painting the walls we want painted. Having never done that before, we decide it would be a fun activity and go past the hardware shop en route. Choosing deep tones and complimentary light ones, each room gets a pot or three of paint assigned to it and stacked into the van with all necessary supplies to actually do the painting.

The HKea is a huge shop and we end up taking a catalogue, sitting in the cafeteria and mapping out all the rooms before we go and look at the displays. Someone from the shops sees this and brings us a shop tablet and helps out with the listings. Thanks to that, once we have chosen most of the furniture, bedding and other items, we can walk around the displays, change a few items in the order and just check out afterwards. Most of the items will be delivered within two days, especially mattresses and bedding which is very useful for us. The only hassle that remains is a lack of kitchen and usable bathrooms. We'll have to get that sorted before we can really enjoy our new home so we are all going to a nearby hotel for the next few nights.

The next few days are a jumble of fun, games and total madness as we learn to paint the walls of the house, get the bathrooms done and get our furniture in too. The guys from HKea sent a five-man building crew to help us set everything up and it was thus done in less than half a day. It's logical but still remarkable how easily professionals do their jobs. Dad and Leyna set us up with a house server to which all the security system is run and it's connected directly to headquarters back in Scotland with a satellite backup too. Dad installed a load of extra detectors and other things in the house, on the roof and in the gardens. This place is a small park with a strangely built tall house in the middle of it so it's quite interesting to set it up security-wise. The gardens are going to need a lot of upkeep as they are so Hayannah offered we just plant them full of endemic trees.

Further preparation of the house will have to wait for when we have time. Dad and Leyna need to leave for Boston and we are starting class on Monday, the day after tomorrow. We take them to the airport, this time in a second had car dad found for us. He somehow managed to get a Lada off-roader for a decent price and that's going to be our new vehicle. Leyna is a little sad to leave but also overjoyed by her soon to be access to the rocket laboratory at MIT. Despite her age, many of her peers there are really looking forward to meeting her and working with the young genius. It's a little strange to me that Hayannah graduated her degree early, Leyna has PhDs and other degrees and I'm here with nothing to my name. It feels almost wrong but, then again, they didn't go through three years of Cross-Gen and more.

After dropping them off, Hayannah and I head home and, for the first time in a long time, it's just the two of us. We light a bunch of scented candles, turn on some nice music and head for the bath together.

I'm not going to go into any extra details but, well, we've had a lot to discover about each other and some of said discovery was done soon after we lit the last candle.

Getting ready for classes and changes

Although it took us the entire to finish setting everything up, Hayannah and I are rather excited to start going to class. In the time we had between Dad leaving and our first classes, a Saturday and a Sunday, we turned our entire house into something resembling a home. Between painting the remaining walls and getting the bathrooms fully done, we spent any remaining time building the last of the furniture and decorating. Hayannah is going to go to her parents' house next month and bring back her things. Even if I wish I could, Dad has made it quite clear he would prefer I don't travel for a little while. We've got to go to the university later, for our first classes and final registration; this would be fine if I wasn't on my period again and feeling horribly unclean. My hormones are still a little off so my periods are not regular at all.

A quick walk to the nearest pharmacy and I have a new, better, menstrual cup. It's certainly not the most comfortable thing to put in but it sure works well. Between that and my ridiculously powerful healing abilities, this day should be fine. Albeit a bit uncomfortable to explain, the gender duality that was created by my hybridisation really makes it easy to understand why women complain about their periods; it's really not a fun thing to live with. Enough about my period, it's strange enough that I have one in the first place, not need to linger on it. We're off to the university soon and that requires a few last bits of preparation, mainly wearing clothing. Hayannah and I have – in the space of a few days – become very comfortable with our home, especially our privacy, and thus don't tend to wear clothes at home. Clothing on fur is generally not the most agreeable anyway so it tends to lead to discomfort which we can easily avoid by being a little less self-conscious. This arrangement started as soon as we had a bed and decided to sleep together in it as we did back in Scotland. Despite us dating, neither she nor I really know anything about couple things. As with anyone our age, we know what happens but that doesn't mean we are at the stage of putting this information into practice. Kisses are one thing, an especially delectable and amazing thing, but anything else is still a little far off I feel. No one really knows what Cross-Gen did to my body in the mountains but it was certainly not a good set of actions considering my uncontrollable fear of being touched in some areas. Add to this the general fear of mistakes and the constant worry of hurting each other because of our strength and reflexes being so much more than humans. Of course, we have discovered some pleasant things already but nothing getting close to PG-18 yet.

Getting back to the topic of going to university, we had to run to campus – not at our normal speed mind you – so as to not miss our registration time. When we made it to campus, no one seemed to care too much about us getting there in rather light clothes considering the winter season and falling snow. I'm wearing modified pants – I even have underwear on today because of my period – and my top is just a long-sleeved woollen jumper. With my tail and ears on full display, the other students rapidly react to our presence. Thankfully, they don't seem to be too pressing contrary to what I had feared; a few people approach us but it's mainly just to welcome us to the university and wish us a good semester. It's a pleasant change of environment from the recent places I've been.

With the student registrar's office being closed, we find the location of the departments we will be studying in and get our registration done there. After many late nights talking about this, we decided that our hybrid minds can deal with a lot more than a single or double major so we are both doing three majors. A little bit of figuring things out lead Hayannah to register into a degree of French, a degree in international communities and management as well as a degree in graphic design. I changed my mind a little and registered in computer science and mechatronics, electronics and civil engineering; pretty much all the basics I need to complement the work of Hayannah and Leyna and thus have all the required skills to build anything. I wanted to add architecture but was told I need civil engineering first. The most difficult part was to negotiate with the head of faculty for each department to allow me to take two years and three majors worth of classes in one semester. They don't believe I'll be able to keep up with the work and the credits but, as it all fits into my schedule, I can do it. Nothing can be difficult enough for it to be impossible. The most difficult part of the entire process was actually when I had to tick both the 'male' and 'female' boxes on my applications and it was not possible. They had to make a few phone calls before it was made possible.

With our various registrations done, the next step is to go purchase a huge stack of textbooks for the classes we registered ourselves into. We won't be needing quite a few of them because Leyna and Dad have a huge digital library and they were in there. Regardless, a decent number still needs to be purchased and this is when I feel a little guilty for always using dad's money. It would be quite a good idea for me to get a job but that's impossible with the absolutely crazy schedule this semester. Hayannah is also a little uncomfortable about just using dad's money but then again, she is theoretically still employed by him.

With campus being rather large, we end up walking through and past a lot of student crowds. Somehow, this led to a number of people asking to chat with us and soon we are completely swamped by very interested students. The most surprising of all of it is that the students are not really being nosy but rather stating that they 'have our backs'. Somehow, somewhere, someone on campus spread the news of us arriving and linked it to the news recording when I explained the torture I had been through. Solidarity is not missing, even in a place where students are not known to care for each other overly much. With a few of these people sticking to us and actually chatting with us, we end up invited to a multitude of pre-semester parties and various study clubs. First, however, we need to get our books and be ready for classes to start.

The various book shops on campus have what we need and, with everything bought, we have three very full book bags which forces us straight home. On the way, Hayannah stops in at a pharmacy but doesn't say why. When I asked her if she is feeling alright, she simply responded that she needed some decent lip balm. It's not a long walk from campus and we make it home in good time. Although it's rather difficult, we have to try not to run too much when we are in town to avoid people being shocked at our speed; that being said, with all the books, it would have been difficult to get up to speed.

A moment of peace and pleasure

—   'Falawk, I'm going to bath.' Says Hayannah as soon as we have locked the door behind us and dropped the books on the table.
—   'Okay
—   And you're going to come with me.' Oh, well I was not expecting that. She is looking at me with a rather interesting smile and a very inviting hand gesture.

— 'I suppose I am. Should I turn the heat on or are you alright?

— Let's make our own heat.'

She said that right before jumping across the room, onto me, and taking my clothes off in a few swift motions. She then raised her arms expectantly and thus requesting I do the same to her. My entire body wants to run away from fear but at the same time – the door is locked, she is my safe person, the one person I really trust – this is something we both wanted for a while now. It's difficult enough to deal with the Post-Traumatic Stress, I don't need to also have fear of the one person I care about enough to live the rest of my life with.

With her clothing off, Hayannah doesn't really seem to know what to do next but, as we often just cuddle, fur against fur, we lie there, in the entryway of the house, cuddling for a few seconds before things take a very delightful turn. Sliding off me and pulling me up, we dash up two floors to our room and then our bathroom, we are soon tussling about kissing while the bath fills with water. Hayannah magically produces a bath bomb and throws it in between two kisses. As two very excited, hormonally active, young adult, hybrids, we soon started discovering things I really thought I would take years to be okay with. With my subconscious fear of everything, the first few minutes are really difficult to enjoy until we really start discovering each other's bodies. It's a good thing I've been keeping my claws and paws in check because, before I really understand what I'm doing, Hayannah guides my hand towards parts of her body I've only ever longed for and never dared touch. The part where this all screeches to a halt is when I have to rapidly deal with my lady monthly issues. As mentioned earlier, I can only praise my ridiculously rapid healing abilities for making my period last hours rather than days. It's also a little silly that I have a period considering the rest of the reproductive parts are not there.

Being intersexed when you were born fully male is quite a leap in self-identity and, I admit, my entire mind and body are still healing from it. Of course, after years of abnormal hormonal intake followed by a rather violent hybridisation, it's to be expected that I would not feel particularly in touch with my body. There has never really been a time when I thought to myself 'Heck yeah, I'm a dude' it's always been pretty complicated and, living in an orphanage with a majority of girls didn't help much at all. I've been trying to figure it out before Hayannah and I get too intimate because it's a little awkward to want to be with her while also not knowing what I want. All in all, I've come to the conclusion that I am what I am and that my hormones are a pain in the neck. However, that's not going to stop me from feeling rather shy when my entire body reacts to her presence and everything become possible.

With the girl problems dealt with and a decent clean later, we get right back to business. From discovering shyly, we seem to have skipped a few gears and gone straight to maximum energy. As soon as she tries something that works on me, I try it on her and vice versa. It's a great way to learn a lot about each other and how our new bodies work. Soon we are splashing in the bath and still playing like the hormonally driven hybrids we are. There is nothing soft about our learning process but it's so enjoyable that I can't complain in any way. And that's going to have to be the end of the details that I will write down considering the probability of my family reading this one day.

After what seems to have been a few hours considering the setting sun, we dry off and get into comfortable clothes before heading down for dinner. In this case, comfortable clothes mean we are both wearing loose warm fleecy dresses that leave good clearance for our tails. Dinner today is going to be a nice, home-made, chicken soup and fresh baked bread. I bought a bread machine because I like bread so much and it's been awesome. We also have a very cool Korean rice cooker that sings when it's done cooking. It's been rather fun making food together as we realised that the temple food is quite similar to Korean traditional dishes thus, we are both more than glad to have it.

Dinner is always a time when we talk and discuss whatever we need to do next.

— 'Well, that was certainly a lot more interesting than I could have expected. You really are an amazing partner Hayannah, I hope you know that.

— It's only normal to make sure you are fully taken care of and to be careful around your fears and traumas. That being said, I think we may end up with a few extra scars if we do it like that each time.

— For sure, I think we may need to keep our hormones under check a little better next time. Regardless, it was amazing and I could certainly do it every day and still think that.

— Same here. In fact, if you're done with your soup, this table is starting to look like a great spot, don't you think?

— Well, now that you mention that, I'll just turn the home security mode to privacy otherwise it will get rather awkward next time we see Dad and Leyna.

— Yes please, I really don't want to have to explain that I'm a huge novice at this and find it all fascinating and intriguing. Also, you'll need to tell me what you like and don't like so that I can get better.

— For now, you've been amazing so just keep going like that and it'll be great.

— Well, enough talking, I'll do the dishes quickly, you get the security system set so that we have a private house.

— Done.'

It doesn't take much longer before we are clearing the table and, if I'm being honest, pretty much every flat surface we can find. We are tussling and playing more than anything else at first but – as with any hormonally induced game – it rapidly turns serious and squeals and yelps can be heard. I'm realising now why Dad said 'This house will give you both the privacy you need,' with a huge wink before leaving.

The First Classes and News

The pleasures of yesterday mean the sleepiness of today and today is the first day of class. Although we could theoretically not go to class until Monday next week, this week, there are special classes for people with crazy schedules. The hardest thing to do now is to make sure we can actually juggle all of our courses. I have not done any of the pre-reading I wanted to because two horny hybrids were far too busy for that, and I'm one of those two. As soon as we reached campus, we had to head to our separate classes and, from there on, it's shoulder to the wheel and grind. In hopes of it serving as a quick way to success, we both have the altered laptops from Leyna that have much more resistant keyboards to allow hybrid speeds without breaking; they are bulky though which is not the best. Saying that, it's a good thing because I'm not as efficient as I would like to be with note taking since I've not been doing any kind of serious studying for a long while; at least not in a classroom.

My first class is a mechatronics lecture followed by a lab in the same subject. It's a four-hour grind with no breaks. Somehow, though, it feels almost restful compared to what I had originally expected. There doesn't seem to be any reason to worry about this course, the teacher is good at explaining things in a nice and clear way. It's really helpful that he is also being deliberately fast with the boring parts and spending extra time on the difficult parts. It really does make it a lot easier to follow along with him. We are immediately learning about the various forms robotics can take, then the usages of programming and the need for a decent amount of knowledge there to be able to apply it here. So, I'll be reading through and practising a lot of Leyna's old coding books if I want to try and keep up with this course and my other ones too.

Come lunch time, it's a quick dash to the building where Hayannah has class and we have just about enough time to kiss, eat lunch and head back to class. We're both holding up a lot better than I expected and I think that, in this context again, being hybrids is giving us the advantage here. I have six more hours of class today and then we want to go to the climbing wall and see how it is there and if they'll let us climb.

Though they are very different in nature, the civil engineering class was boring at first and then took off quite well as opposed to the last class of the day, a remedial physics class which I will no longer need to go to but that had been scheduled in case. It turns out my physics knowledge didn't go anywhere and I'm still more than capable of learning and solving most problems. Hayannah was waiting for me just outside of class with our sports bags, she had time to go home and collect them before my last class concluded. Leading the way, she holds my hand and walks us to the large sports hall from which we can already hear the screech of shoes and slams of rackets. It takes us only a minute to get from my class building to the hall and then it's a stop in the changing rooms and we are off to the climbing wall. It's at this moment that I realised how progressive and liberal this university must be; there are non-gendered changing rooms and showers which are all in the form of private cubicles. We take one of them and quickly get changed into our well-adapted sports clothes.

With tails swaying and ears flicked back to reduce the ambient noise, we walk towards the wall and are immediately the cause of more than one misses in the badminton sets. They are all far too interested in the two hybrids to focus on their coordination. The coach at the wall asks if we are willing to do a few tests before he lets us climb and, when I ask why, he just says, 'because I've been dreaming of watching a world record be broken for years'. He has Hayannah do the tests first and then it's my turn. We start with a grip strength test: picking up weights with thumb and forefinger, then adding more weight until we can't. Hayannah stops at 175 kg and I make it to 220 kg. This is enough to have the entire gym staring. We then repeat that exercise but this time squeezing the handle between ring and middle finger. This is a far more difficult exercise and we stop at 50 kg and 60 kg respectively. The next and last test he asks is for a vertical jump and catch of a pair of rings. They start at two metres and we end up with Hayannah beating me at 4m50 where I only get 3m95. It's fun and all that but the crowd and videos are a little less fun.

We then get shown the basics of lead climbing, bouldering and speed climbing before being let loose into the crowd. Everyone wants to become our friends and help us out but the coach soon calms them down asking for us to be given space to train too. As an end-of-day activity, lead climbing is certainly fun and interesting. We start off with the basics under the guidance and counsel of a very kind climber by the name Aila. They are a very soft-spoken and kind person who is more than willing to explain things a few times. However, that's not really necessary and we are soon all three climbing together. Starting from a 5a, we end the session on 7c. This is apparently a long way beyond most of the climbers who come to this gym regularly and thus surprises our new friend. Aila offers to go out for dinner after the session and we thus head out together after a quick shower.

Although I want to be on my guard around pretty much everyone, it's really difficult not to be fond of someone who is just permanently kind like our new friend. They are being very polite around both of us and even trying to guard us so that our tails don't sway into people as we walk through a rather crowded street. They really are taking every measure possible to make Hayannah and I comfortable, what a kind person.

Our meal consists of a great pile of pilaf rice and meat at a slightly unappealing restaurant that turns out to be some of the nicest foods we've had in a long time. This reminds me of the various experimental dishes I made after getting home from the temple. It mostly reminds me that there is more to eating than feeding my ever-demanding body the energy source it needs. It's almost as though – be it because of the lovely company or the quality and taste of the food – I finally appreciating eating for the first time in a long while. When pudding comes, it's in the form of ice cream on waffles and an absolute shower of maple syrup on it. As cliché as that may sound, it's as lovely as it is sweet.

With dinner done, Aila needs to head home and so do we but, before we do, we exchange numbers and promise to meet up again soon. Hayannah and I head home through the parks and enjoy the night walk like the adorable couple I think we are. Holding hands, swinging our arms and tails, just enjoying life as it should be. It's at this point that I start to wonder if things are not too peaceful but then again, it's pretty nice to just live in the moment a bit. As we turn onto our street and then up to our house, I get a call from Leyna.

— 'Hey lovebirds, how are you feeling today? How was the first day of class?

— It was nice and interesting even if it feels like it is a little slow for my hybrid brain.' Replies Hayannah before I add my response.

— 'It was quite cool actually; mechatronics is fun but I'll have to pick up your coding textbooks before I can really deal with that class. The civil engineering class is also pretty decent. How about you Sis?

— The lab people are really great, the fact that I'm bringing a few patents with me and that they get to co-sign one of them really helped me earn a lot of respect. Although I'm the youngest in a mile radius here, it's still quite a nice environment.

— That's great to hear. How is that jet engine patent coming along?

— Done and confirmed. We patented the process, the tools required and the actual schematics and product. Funny enough, Elon Muzk contacted the lab minutes after the patent was released asking for a conference with us to negotiate using it.

— Leyna, that's incredible, well done! You're really awesome, I hope you know that.' Says Hayannah as we walk through the front door. The house 'wakes up' and so the call gets transferred onto the home system.

— 'Thank you big sis. It gets better, though; I'll be travelling to Quebec City for a conference in three weeks. So, it should be easy for me to come over for a few days.

You did leave my room untouched by your nightly affaires, right?' Wait, but the house was on privacy mode, how does she know. 'The privacy mode says it all big bro, don't worry, though, I don't care and would love a niece or nephew.

— 'Leyna, I'm flying to Korea in two and a half weeks for nearly a month, I'm going to be missing you this time. I'm sorry little sis.' Says Hayannah promptly changing subject.

— 'Don't worry about it, there will be other opportunities. Or I'll just get there the night before.'

Our conversation goes on another short while before we sign off, put some ambient music on and go to the bathroom to get clean and into nightwear, in our case nothing. We barely make it there that all the energy and desire from yesterday come racing back up and we are immediately forced to set privacy mode into the default and then proceed with our night. It's not as though we plan any of this but it does tend to happen a lot and always unexpectantly. The only hassle is that we must cut short to be able to do homework reading.

What Should I Say About This

From classes to homework and lots of climbing, Hayannah and I had a few very busy weeks. Thank goodness there is a week and a half break starting Friday. Hayannah had to change her return flight and will only be gone for two weeks rather than a month. Leyna is arriving Thursday and Hayannah flies out the next morning. We've been seeing Aila a lot, they are very interested in the entire concept of hybridisation and asked if it would be possible, one day for them to become a hybrid. Asking dad about this, the answer was simply that I would have to vet the person but it is possible so long as they have not passed the age of 21. Anyone older than that will have a much harder time adapting to the mutations and could thus die from the process. The fact that Aila is 18 thus helps quite a bit. They started university at 16 after graduating high school at 14 but taking a year to access and get funding. Aila is really interesting and, interestingly, is also doing aeronautics and knew who Leyna was because of her publications. It seems as though they have been chatting as well because he asked me for her personal number saying he had her permission over email but that I needed to allow it too. Dad and Leyna are trusting me to approve or not the people who we allow into the family's inner circle.

Today, at climbing, I gave Aila my little sister's number as well as the home-approved messaging app. It's an encrypted system dad made years ago that our entire home system is based on. It allows for full-quality communication, over low network, while being impossible to crack. The only way I can describe Aila at the moment of hitting 'save' on their phone is with the word 'ecstatic'. They actually bounced around like a little child and then immediately called Leyna. When she picked up, I only needed to overhear the first few words to understand this was the last step in a process for them two. Although I don't think my sister would just start dating someone, she is certainly being very kind to Aila and speaking with what I call her 'cute voice'.

After that climbing session, Aila, Hayannah and I headed to the shops to get a few things. We've been doing quite a few things with Aila recently, not because of anything other than the pleasant company. We made other friends too but, somehow, Aila seems to be the most stable and caring of them all. Shopping together rapidly became a habit after, they were so careful around our tails and sensitivity going to eat out on our first encounter.

We get the usual, a lot of rice, some vegetables and a significant amount of meat in various forms. The best thing Aila taught us in recent days was the reopening of the farmer's market next month. This comes with the added bonus of being able to buy moose meat in very large quantities. Although I don't always want to admit it, meat is really the base of my diet these days and it's allowing me to gain even more strength and somehow also making me lose the tiny amount of body fat I had. However, there is one major downside of eating like this, if I ever have to survive off the land, hunting would be my only option and I'm not sure I could face that. Obviously, if it's the only choice then maybe, though I would rather learn about all the edible roots, leaves and other plant-related things.

With our shopping done, Hayannah offered for Aila to come over and have dinner at our place. They have not actually been to the house yet and thus will need to be electronically vetted in and for that I call my sister.

— 'Hey big bro, what are you up to?
— We're heading home from shopping with your crush. Could you vet them into the home system please, they are coming over for dinner.' I say with a sidewards glance at Aila to see them blushing a dark crimson.
— 'They are really cute and in case you forgot, I'm old enough anyway.' Replies Leyna with a falsely angry voice. Although we've all been missing our birthdays, she is now legally an adult and I'm almost internationally adult. 'They are vetted into the system.
— Thanks a lot, and if you're free. Want to video call us later so you can be virtually there?
— Yes please.
— Alright, call in about a quarter. Love you Sis.
— Love you back big bro.'

We get to the gates of the house and Aila asks, 'are you two house-sharing with other students or just the landlords?' To which I have to, somehow, respond without sounding like a rich entitled git. When Hayannah comes in to save me by saying that my dad owns the place, Aila just smiles and says, 'Considering his patents, I should not be surprised but I still am.' It's true that Dad has amassed a decent amount of wealth over the years but the majority of it comes from selling his research back when I was a kid. Also, mum's life insurance apparently paid out a significant amount once dad 're-alived'.

Dinner takes us a while to prepare and, Leyna having called in, we end up playing games at the same time rather than solely focussing on cooking. It's great fun and we are, in due time, sitting around the table, Leyna on video call, projected on the wall, all enjoying our dinners and finishing off our round of a popular digital board game. It's been a lovely evening and Leyna managed to really enjoy her night for the first time in a while, according to her. She says that, although the lab people are amazing, as she is still underage, she can't go and party with them so it makes it a little too difficult for her to really make friends. She has thus been spending way too much time working and studying rather than enjoying any of her free time. Dad's been totally off communications for a few weeks as he is preparing something huge that he doesn't want us to know about. Just as Leyna was saying that, he requested to join our call.

— 'Hey kids, hey Hayannah, hello Aila nice to meet you. Sorry for barging in, I have very big news for you.

— Hey Dad.' I say almost perfectly in sync with Leyna.

— 'Hello daddy Rogue, hope you are well.' Says Hayannah.

— 'Nice to meet you Professor Rogue.' Says Aila with a small head bow.

— 'As I said, big news, this is mostly for you, Falawk. The Cross-Gen centre in France has finally been cleared. We managed to organise a very tactical strike and got all the kids out.

— Is this what you were organising dad?

— In part son, it's been a long process to get the military, the police and everyone to agree on the best way to proceed. When we originally made contact, through the anti-terrorism cell, they sent out three kids and shot them.

— They did what?' Stops Leyna with a very angry voice.

— 'They acted like the terrorists they are, they killed people to prove that they have the resolve to hold their hostages. It took a very specialised team of people to infiltrate and get the kids out. All the researchers are now in a maximum-security prison and being interrogated.' I can't believe they would go to those kinds of lengths just to hide their idiocy.

— 'Have there been any more hybrids?' It is the only thing I think of asking.

— 'None yet but, as you know, they messed with the hormones a lot so they may reveal themselves in coming weeks. I've been working around the clock with the French government to have all the kids hosted in low-cost housing with 24/7 medical supervision.

— Please just give them the freedom to be with each other too.

— They already have that son, don't worry. Their identities are being verified and we are getting many of them back to their families if they want to go. For those who don't, most of their countries, especially the European ones, have accepted to take them under legal tutelage and get them into school and so on.

— That's great. Thanks Dad.' It's crazy to think that they really managed to get everyone out and Cross-Gen still never made another hybrid. What an absolute bunch of idiots.

— 'Professor, have you had any news on the kids who were taken out before? I heard that many didn't stay for the full program.' Asks Aila.

— 'You can just call me Piet or Pieter, no need to use titles Aila. As for the people who were sent out, we're looking through the digital archives at the lab to try and find out but currently we don't know.

— So, no trace of Jenny right dad?' Asks Leyna.

— 'Nothing yet but we're looking. I'll keep you up to date with as much information as possible. We're going to be organising a raid on the lab in the Himalayas soon too. That is just taking a lot more work because we need to coordinate with China, Nepal, Mongolia and India so it's complicated.'

Our conversation goes on for long enough that it's far too late to send Aila home alone so, with her permission, they sleep over in Leyna's room. For some reason, it really doesn't bother me to have them staying over regardless of only knowing them for a few weeks. Somehow, somewhere, I just started to trust them and from there on out it's just been getting better. It's as though, because of the lack of general judgement and the constant kindness, and, although it's hard to admit, the affection for my sister, Aila just feels like a good person.

Once we have all wished each other good night, it's off to sleep time, we do, after all, have class tomorrow again. Just because we like hang around until late and have fun doesn't mean we get to skip classes. Hayannah and I have our first exams as soon as she is back from Korea so that's going to be quite a thing, I'm sure. Nonetheless, it's not going to stop us from enjoying our time with our new friends and our student life as much as possible. It's certainly not going to stop us from enjoying the coming holidays and all the fun that's going to be bringing us.

It's Cute but Still

The week came and went way too fast and it's now time for me to pick up my little sister from the airport. Aila offered to go and I nearly fell for it but decided to pull the over-protective older brother card and say, 'I'll drive.' This is a partial apology to handle getting my sister home before she goes off on her own adventures, but also a great time for me to chat with Aila. They didn't mind at all and just got in the car with me and we are off to the airport with Leyna landing in a few minutes.

— 'So, Aila, I'm sure you figured me out enough to know that I have ulterior motives for driving you to get my sister. Do you mind if we have a bit of a serious talk?

— Nope, of course, we can and yes I figured you want to have that kind of talk.

— It's just a request actually. I want my sister to be happy and safe, that is not an easy task in the current state of world affaires and especially not for us hybrids.

— That's perfectly logical. I would expect no less from a loving older brother. And, as for being hybrids, well, I've been thinking about it since you guys were on TV the first time, I've kind of fell in love with the idea. I was wondering if I can become one too.

— I suspect you will do great, you're a really nice person. As for becoming a hybrid, there is a possibility but you'll need to speak with my dad. Also, you'll need to do it soon because of your age.

— Does it only work on younger people?

— Not exactly but it seems to not have any effect on people over a certain age. Dad could only test it so much so we don't know exactly what that age is.

— Then I'll need to ask the professor for his opinion and also, maybe, talk to my parents about it. It's not like they care what I do actually, I've not spoken to them for years.

— Check with whom you need, just don't forget, you'll have to go to Rogue Mansion, as in our house in Scotland, that's where the labs are.

— I'm sure that'll be fine.

— One other thing about this, why do you want to become a hybrid? I mean, what's your real reason?

— The real answer to that is far too kitschy but, to be honest, because I want to be like Leyna, Hayannah and you. You three are so awesome and free and able to do so many cool things.'

Our conversation goes on like this for a long while until we reach the airport, park the car and get to the arrivals area just as Leyna is walking through. She is proudly showing off her hybrid form so I drop my hoody and let my tail wag a lot more under my long skirt. She drops her suitcase, runs and jump-hugs Aila. Part of me wants to be jealous until she just as quickly hugs me.

Before I know it, I'm playing taxi with them two in the back while I drive us back home. They have been chatting and messing about for a good part of the trip before I feel the need to pester them and say, 'I'll look away, you can kiss now.' That's enough to get them both to change skin tone completely. Leyna says, in our family language, 'I'm planning to be a lot less innocent than that older brother.' My own sister, my pure and kind-hearted little sister, telling me she plans on sleeping with my friend. That's a little awkward even for me. I'll need to warn Hayannah that there will be a ban on the second floor while Leyna is home. There are many reasons why I would and maybe should stop them but, regardless of how valid my arguments are, my sister looks really happy and that's all that matters.

By the time we reach home, they have managed to remain good and innocent at which point I park, hand Aila the keys and tell them to go on a date. Hayannah gets a nice hug and a suitcase is dropped off before Aila and Leyna disappear down the drive again. Aila says he 'knows a spot' and we all know what that can mean, it's the universal term for 'I know a really cool and amazing place; let me show you.'

The two of them being off for a little while, Hayannah and I take this opportunity to enjoy our last night together for a fortnight and make popcorn, order steak dinner and watch a movie. Hayannah then pulls one of the hottest lines in our relationship time: 'I'm off to bath. And you are going to join me.' That's when our evening took a much more ferocious turn. Be it because we are enjoying our privacy or because we won't be seeing each other for two weeks, this just feels so much more fervent and energetic than even our craziest moments. Hayannah is leading a lot and being quite clear about what she wants to do and receive, something that she is usually rather shy about. She has really learnt to deal with all parts of me and has become excellent at making sure I'm fully satisfied. With her being straight and all, I was worried she might struggle with my intersex nature but instead, and I quote, she loves me for who I am regardless of what's in my pants.

At some time in the early morning, long after Hayannah and I fell asleep I'm woke by a catering noise. It's only when I hear Leyna's laugh and a soft Aila's voice telling her to be quiet that I know they are back. That's my queue to fall asleep again and ignore any sound I hear from Leyna's room.

The next morning, rather earlier than our body clocks would have liked, I am taking Hayannah to the airport. She is flying with nothing but the clothes on her back and a small bag. His plan is to save on this trip so that she can have five boxes on her way back. In her mind, in spite of what I say, we are going to be living here in Canada for a long while. I don't mind the idea at all but I just really don't know if I think this is our life location now. It's as though, because of our choice of study location and the fact that my dad bought us a house here, Canada and specifically Quebec have become our new home.

By the time we get to the airport, I have to wake Hayannah up, get her to the baggage check-in and then help her to customs too. As per usual regulations, I'm not allowed to go in with her but the security agent is very kind and allows me to walk-carry her to the actual customs agent, she is falling asleep on my shoulder the whole time, though. The agent checks her passport and smiles at us and tells me in crisp British English, 'We'll look after her sir, don't worry.' It's really kind of them to say and I give her a last kiss before seeing her through the gates. Almost immediately, she calls me and says she loves me and then she is off to board her plane. We nearly didn't make it in time, they had to move the schedule of the flight up because of the current struggles in the Pacific between the two Koreas.

Owing to Leyna's intervention, Hayannah has a satellite transmitter in her bag that allows her to constantly be trackable and gives her the opportunity to communicate whenever she wants. There is now nothing to worry about; or at least that's what I'm telling myself so that I can avoid remembering the times when I was captured before flights. The most important thing to remember is actually that, regardless of anything, Cross-Gen is having to be a lot more discreet now that their French operation was taken down. Of course, we don't know what the backlash for that is going to be but we can only hope that they will not take it out on people who have nothing to do with them.

It's now time for me to head home and go and deal with my sister and her partner being lovey-dovey when I can't be.

What is it this time?

It's time for a party

Hayannah having been in Korea for almost two weeks now, she is flying back tomorrow and has already shipped a few boxes on top of the five she is bringing back on the plane. Believe it or not, the cost of the extra luggage actually worked out cheaper than shipping her things. She did, however, request that we find her a piano because her mommy won't let her take their one. This, somehow, became a mission for Aila as they really love music. They have been studying it alongside their normal studies since middle school and can play guitar and piano rather very well. The only thing left to do now is for me to hand them my card and watch and see what they end up bringing home. As she has been ever since arriving here in Quebec, Leyna is stuck to Aila and is thus going with for this excursion. My little sister has been showing me a whole new side of her personality I could not have guessed existed. She has made it very clear that I am to accept Aila as part of the family because she is truly fond of them.

After quite a few phone calls, Aila and Leyna have finally convinced me to let them add to the piano fund – so did Dad – resulting in a rapid need for moving things around in our ground-floor room. They ended buying a full-sized Steinway and Sons grand piano. I can't begin to imagine how Hayannah will react when she finds out. It's as I'm moving the last shelf of books out of the way that they arrive with the delivery person from the music shop. The piano must weigh in at nearly 500 kilograms says the delivery person. The poor lad was not expecting to be delivering to two hybrids, though. Leyna hops into the van and grabs one end while I get the other – off we go with a piano. It's heavy and awkward but, thanks to our continuous training, this doesn't actually feel so bad. We walk it through the front door, barely squeezing it in and then set it down waiting for the delivery guy to help us bolt the feet on right and check the tuning. We ask that it be tuned into Verdi's A, at 432 hertz, because it's a little les aggressive on the ears; something very important for us hybrids.

The piano delivery person helps with the final tuning and then is off, leaving us just enough time to quickly get some shopping done before everything closes for the night. This rapidly leads us into a controlled rush as we get bags and containers ready before hopping back in the car and going to the shop. Shopping with my sister is always a lot of fun as we take our hybrid senses and use them to mess with people. We'll, for example, just talk in very soft voices but perfectly understand and hear each other. It's even worse when we do this over multiple isles. Aila is not the least surprised when, for the fifth time, Leyna asked me to bring something, as if she is thinking out loud, and I appear with it or vice versa.

Our shopping takes us well until closing time and we are kindly but definitely asked to finish up and leave. From here, we head home, make dinner and breakfast and then it's sleeping time. I need to pick up Hayannah at 7 in the morning so my little sister clearly stated that she'll be sleeping. Aila and her have been very close but, in many ways, very innocent too. I know they kiss but, unless they are hiding it very well, I don't think they've stepped into any further realms.

As soon as we got home, with a lot of energy spent to go as fast as possible, Leyna and I race to prepare dinner and breakfast while Aila gives us background music from the ground floor. He's certainly a good pianist but he mainly plays classical music, something I'm not the most appreciative of. Generally speaking, I prefer folk music and independent artists who fall under the greater categories of post-rock and traditional music. With Leyna far in the lead on breakfast, I up my game and start actually going full speed. This is something I've only been daring recently as it requires a lot of strength control owing to the massive muscle power I can access. To be fair, Leyna can do the same but she is maybe ten or fifteen percent slower than me at full burst. Giving me just enough time to finish preparing all my ingredients, I roll one kimbap with each hand and, benefiting greatly from my ambidextrous nature, produce a full meal worth within a couple of minutes. We decided to eat Korean food tonight so I made one of the quickest and nicest kinds I know.

After a nice meal, savouring both the food and my thirty-second victory at the speed-run, I head up to the master bedroom tidy it up, clean it and prepare space for her to bring in her things. This takes enough of my remaining energy that I end up quite sweaty. Calling for a nice long shower, at least ten minutes, I head there and wash all my fur, hair and then have to dry it all off. Fur is great but for the drying it off part, that's always more complicated. Saying that, it means that, at least, I'll not dirty the fresh linen in the nest and will also feel nice and fresh tomorrow morning to go and pick up my lovely partner. Speaking of, I've been wondering if it's not time I ask her if she would like to be my wife. We've never spoken about that but it just feels logical considering she became a hybrid to be with me. Our relationship is already developed a lot further than I would have expected considering the massive breaks we had because of distance and my capture.

Let's Enjoy This Peace

This morning, before even sparrow fart, it was time to wake up, grab breakfast and pack it in before heading to the airport to get Hayannah. I can watch her arrive thanks to the awesome tech Leyna gave her. It's pretty fun to have three-dimensional location data for someone in a plane. It's as though the system wants to constantly tell me that she is travelling a little too fast for it to be normal. Furthermore, the constant details tell me that she'll be landing long before I can get to the airport, which is fine because of the customs and baggage delay but it may take me a minute to find parking.

Arriving closer to the airport, things only get a little more complicated. There is a huge traffic jam and it doesn't seem to be going anywhere any time soon. Although I wish I could take a detour, the GPS is telling me that the traffic is backed up on all roads leading to the airport. My first reaction to this is to ping Hayannah and ask her if everything is alright and then to ping Dad, who is back in Scotland, to ask for a bit of extra information. He has far higher access than what he should have.

— 'Hey Son, I've got some good and some bad news. Good news is, Hayannah will be able to land safely. Bad news is that their flight is being diverted to Quebec airport in Quebec City. If the footage I'm seeing is anything to go by, they have evacuated the airport near you for some reason.

— Do you know what the reason is?

— No idea, I'm sifting through the cameras as we speak. Ah. There it is.

— What?

— I'm going to guess it's a terrorist attack of some kind. There are three groups of heavily armed men pointing automatic weapons at some shop workers and passengers.

— Oh, hostage situation or hold-up? Why do I have such bad luck with airports?'

We chat a little longer before I put the car into four-wheel mode, get myself through the traffic and over the lane barrier before speeding off the other direction. It's going to take me nearly an hour to get to Quebec City, thus making Hayannah wait for me a little because she'll be landing soon. It's nothing a little driving over the speed limit can't fix but, saying that, I'd rather not get a speeding fine just because I want to see my partner so badly. After all, love can't be a valid reason to cause an accident on the road.

I make it to the airport just in time to see Hayannah walk through the arrivals gate with a trolly piled high with boxes. I parked in the quick pick-up zone and dash to get her and the boxes. The hug she gives me is magical and the ensuing kiss even better. It's crazy how much I missed her and it was only two weeks. We get the boxes into the car and, just as we're about to set off, Leyna calls in asking if everything is alright. Dad told her about the situation at the airport and she was worried that Hayannah would be waiting for ages.

Hayannah and I head towards home, stopping on the way at a lovely frozen lake to eat our breakfast and enjoy a beautiful rising sun. This, to my surprise, is the moment my lovely partner chooses to ask me the question I've been dying to ask: 'Should we get married?' She says it in such a loving and yet calm way by which she asks me this. Obviously – I say yes – I really want to spend my life with her. This leads to a long discussion during which we magically hash out all the difficult details. We'll get married in Canada, formally that is, invite her parents and her older brother, invite my dad and uncle as well as a few of her friends. Because of my traditionalist desires, I ask her if I could first propose to her, correctly, with a ring and all those lovely things. She agrees to this but also says that, because I want to do that, we should make it a very personal and special moment.

There are so many more things we want to talk about but getting home and actually letting Hayannah enjoy the party we organised for her is probably much more important at this exact moment. We get back into the car after a long and soft lingering kiss, one so soft it brings butterflies and tickles all over. The trip home is a fast one and we just take the time to chat about the various fun things that have happened over the past weeks and what we've been up to. Although we were having daily calls, it's somehow more fun to talk about it like this, in the car, even the details we already know. Hayannah tells me that her parents, having not seen her in person for a while, were rather surprised by the energy and happiness she portrays these days. They said that – regardless of her choice to become a hybrid not being their favourite – they can only admire her new path as she is finally really happy. For the first time, she told them about the moral struggles she had faced in her years at university as well as the years in high and middle school. She tells me that they didn't really know how to react when she told them about the constant pressure having hurt her and how, by the importance of her role in finding me, she finally felt as though she was being appreciated for the work she does. On top of this she also saw her friends and many of them were really interested in her new life as a hybrid and she was even asked to join a popular social media app to post pictures and stories about her life as a hybrid.

By the time we make it home, it's past dark and there is a lot of hushed activity in the house. Even if we had a bit of a difficult time convincing dad to let there be a party at the house, he ended up saying 'Falawk, it's your house, you can do whatever you want, just be safe' which Leyna heard and took as 'go ahead, make a huge party'. She organised the entire event and got quite a few interesting things set up. Mainly, our climbing friends, Aila helped there, some class mates of Hayannah's, some of mine and then some of Leyna's lab friends. She is managing to make friends a lot easier here as, for some reason, they don't see her age as a factor at all. It's a little silly for them to be hushing their voices considering the two people arriving are hybrids with extremely powerful hearing but, in order to help the surprise, I give Hayannah my headphones and play her a song I 'thought she would like'. It's a terrible excuse but it works.

Carrying the boxes in front of her, she doesn't see the movement in the main room as she heads up the stairs while swaying to the music. I smile at Leyna and help with the last boxes. As I get into the room, Hayannah takes off the headphone and, in one swift motion takes off everything she was wearing beckoning me towards her. Well, this is a little awkward.

— 'Darling, I would love to make the most of you but, well, I have to spoil it now.
— Oh, you mean the fifteen people in the other room, the twenty in the kitchen and five in the pantry? I know they are there but I'm sure you can be fast if I ask nicely.
— Wait, did the music not help and yes, I can.'

Our conversation is cut short when I hear Leyna's voice up the stairs, in the family language saying, 'Hurry up but don't worry I'll keep them busy.' Damned us hybrids and our ears. Hayannah shreds through my clothing and, before I know how to react, she is on top of me playfully nibbling at my ear. I'll not be going into any more details about those five minutes but it's safe to say they don't disappoint. In light of the party-to-come, we decide to just clean off rapidly, slip into comfy clothes and head down.

— 'That took you long enough, I'm sure you can get changed faster than that' says Khaled, one of my classmates.

— 'I'm pretty sure there was more to it than that bro.' Adds Yvann, one of Hayannah's classmates.

— 'Boys, leave them alone, I'm pretty sure Hayannah doesn't appreciate that kind of talk.' Defends Judy, one of Leyna's lab friends.

— 'Well, either way, who wants punch, it's a special version made with real Canadian liquor.' Asks Abby, a climbing friend. Somehow Leyna really managed to organise it so that we have everything and so that everything is also kept safe. There are special compounds in the drinks that will turn fluorescent pink if anything unsavoury is added to them.

— 'I could certainly use more snacks, if I knew there would be this many people, I would have prepared more treats.' Says Nell, another one of Hayannah's classmates while guiding Hayannah off to the snacks table.

— 'Well, mate, there goes your bird. She sure is a wonderful partner for you, you two really look good together. When are you getting married?' Asks Zalfos, one of the professors whom I met at climbing.

— 'Actually, I've been wondering that too. With all the chaos you keep facing Falawk, maybe it would be good to tie the knot.' Says Elann, reminding us all of the lovely events I've been living the past few years.

— 'Yeah, good point guys. It's time you two become the first worldwide family of hybrids. I know that Leyna and Falawk are family but this would allow all the magazines to imagine their kids and so on.' Adds Silane smiling at the idea. It's rather frustrating to think about it but I'm sure the tabloids will have a blast the moment we announce we are married.

— 'Well, if you lot let Falawk talk, he may be able to answer you all.' Says Line, finally saving me from the interrogation.

— 'We'll see guys, don't worry, you'll all be made aware in due time when it's going to happen.' I finally manage to reply.

We keep chatting like that for hours into the night before anyone is ready to head off home. Hayannah still hasn't even see her piano at this point which leads to a lovely silence as I walk her down the stairs and show it to her. Of course, at that moment, everyone asks for her to play something and so, regardless of her current state, she decides to go into a full recital. It's such a lovely, peaceful moment, I can hope for but one thing and that is for it not to end too soon.

Well, That Was Short-lived

It's been a few days since the party and I've just dropped Leyna off at the airport. Now it's a case of rush home, drop off the car and get to campus. It's time to get back to the crazy grind of my studies so that I can validate this semester. It's all well and good to have had a two-week break, the grind doesn't stop for anyone and especially not for people like me. There is no rest for the crazy students who want to batch through as many classes as possible.

As soon as I'm on campus and in class, Hayannah messages me to my wristband: 'check the news'. That's not a good sign. I'm about to open the news when the professor stops the class and announces we all need to watch a news brief. The prim minister of Canada comes on and immediately starts with:

'Dear Canadians, we are under attack. In fact, the entire world is. An unknown foe has launched hundreds of missiles into the upper atmosphere. We are yet to determine the nature of these weapons and what they are targeted at but

And just like that the transmission stops. The professor then, without seeming anywhere near as phased as most of the class, states that we need to head to the nearest shelters.

A call to Hayannah later and we are both running to the house at full blast. Aila is going to join us there. They don't have anywhere better to go and it's actually closer than the shelters the university has access to. We quickly head into the tunnel and bar off the outside access before dashing into the house and getting some supplies. As I'm about to run down the stairs dad calls in and forces the pick-up.

— 'Hello you two, you can stop running around, those weapons are from Cross-Gen.' He says in a far too calm voice.
— 'How is that a relaxing piece of information?' Asks Hayannah.
— 'Because they can't harm you, you're both already hybrids. Their lab in the Himalayas is about to be raided

and, as a last resort, they shot the key to hybridisation into the atmosphere as a biochemical weapon.

— So, you mean that they manage to synthesis it and replicate enough to turn the entire planet into hybrids?' I ask not believing the simpleness of that after the years of torture I went through to end up as I am today.

— 'No, if my calculation is correct, it will only affect future births and only about ten to twenty percent of them. It could possibly affect past Cross-Gen patients, though.' For some reason this still doesn't measure me and that's when I figure it out, Dad is dealing with it already, that's why he wants us to just relax.

— 'What have you done dad? What's going on?

— Well, if you must know, I'm currently in Mongolia speaking, in a military operation truck less than a hundred kilometres away from the lab. They are about to bring down the last of the researchers they captured and I'm about to see the man, my ex-colleague, who caused the death of my wife and who tortured my son.' That explains a lot. Again, for some reason my mind just remains calm at this news but it still makes my body react in some way.

— 'Just be safe please. And what can we expect from the bombs?

— Nothing more than what they have already done, they just exploded as we were speaking. The biochemical compound will now seep into everything and anything organic or water-based. The Indian special forces tried to intervene in time to prevent the bombs from actually going off but I guess there must have been a dead-man switch on them in case we capture Martin.' How is he so calm? It's becoming annoying.

— 'Dad, how are you constantly so calm about all of this? What is going on that you're not saying?' I don't mean it but my voice is getting angry.

— 'I'm not calm, I'm beyond exhausted, I've not slept in three days and I've been having to run a lot of the operations because the countries here don't talk to each other. I'm just tired son, nothing else is happening in. I can't be angry yet; my worst enemy is about to be brought before me.' Damned, he really does sound dead tired.

I don't have time to keep talking to Dad, Aila just got through the door and looks rather freaked out. Hayannah is about to help calm them but, announcing its presence, a yellow alarm goes off in the house with a synthetic voice, based on Leyna's, stating, 'Beware, biochemical compounds detected.' Just how safe did they make this place when they set up the security I wonder. It's time for a call with Leyna to ask her how things are on her side of the world. When I call her, she responds very fast with 'I'm fine, I know what's going on, can't talk now I'm busy hacking international communication satellites so that Dad can make an announcement to the entire world.' It's still surprising how she nonchalantly says things like that and then just hangs up.

We turn on the projector in the dining room and open up a major television provider just in time to see their feed go static and then dad appears. He looks as tired as he sounded on the phone. He's in a reasonably well-lit tent of some kind and looking straight at the camera.

'Dear citizens of the world, as most of you know, there were weapons in the atmosphere a until a few minutes ago. These were biochemical weapons launched by the company Cross-Gen. In those weapons was a very specific compound known commonly as "the key to hybridisation" and, after its release onto the world, it will integrate itself into all of your DNAs by means of messenger RNA. This means that there is no cure, no problem to expect and nothing you can do to avoid having it. Currently, I am unsure of the effects this will have on people but I can state one thing for certain, there will be a ten to twenty percent chance of any future children being born hybrids. The reason I am the one announcing this to you all is to also announce that I, Professor Rogue, pledge to do as much as I can to help any future hybrids. You can also expect to see a lot of teens and young adults display minor changes should they have been a part of the test subjects at

He adds a few more details before the streams are recovered by the official media who immediately respond to the information. There is a major amount of information being shared on social media such as Birdy and Write-it where people have entire political debates about my dad's role in the existence of hybrids, the role I, Falawk, have to play in regards to the possible new hybrids and more.

We'll Never Be Alone Again

University has been closed for three weeks due to snow and the bioweapon. It's opening for the first time again today and we've been so busy dealing with everything that I can't even remember what lectures I have this week.

Because of my role as the first hybrid, a lot of national and international media have been contacting me to ask how I feel about the fact that there will be many more hybrids soon.

I keep responding that there is no real way of know when and if such children really will be born but, today, it was proven. In a hospital in Southern Ireland, a baby was born with hybrid eyes. The infant still looks perfectly human though so they might only have eyes unless it develops later.

Dad also agreed to help Aila become a hybrid so our friend if off to Scotland with Leyna next month. They are going to be there long enough for him to start his first mutations with the adequate medical supervision. Leyna is qualified enough to go through the entire hybridisation process but, to avoid any hassles she still revers to Dad for this operation.

Hayannah and I have been dreading the return to campus because there is a rather large online community of hybrid haters that formed after the attacks. I'm not worried about our ability to defend against physical attacks but the risk of verbal attacks is far too high. We get our bags ready and head to campus.

Barely have we set foot on campus that a huge group of people forms around us. They are all saying things like 'we're with you,' 'don't worry, we're here for you' and so on. They are all being genuinely kind with us and really showing their support. From this and the news of more babies being born with hybrid eyes, I can only think one thing:

'We are never going to be alone again.'

To be continued in *Hybridia*